Can Do, Missy Charlie

CAN DO,
MISSY CHARLIE

Barbara Brooks Wallace

Illustrated by Marvin Friedman

Follett Publishing Company
Chicago

Other Books by Barbara Brooks Wallace

ANDREW THE BIG DEAL
CLAUDIA
VICTORIA

Manufactured in the United States of America.

ISBN 0–695–80444–8 Trade binding
ISBN 0–695–40444–X Titan binding

Library of Congress Catalog Card Number: 73–90054

First Printing

For my sister, Connie

The Place: China
The Time: The 1930s

ONE

THE first earsplitting roar from the smokestack of their ocean liner surprised Charlotte and Christene as they were playing a boring game of shuffleboard on the game deck. It was boring because Christene was way ahead, as usual.

She darted toward the iron stairway that led to the upper deck. "Race you, Charlie!" she called out, bounding up the steps two at a time. By the time Charlotte came thumping up breathlessly from behind to join her, she had already climbed on the lowest rung of the deck railing, and was leaning over, squinting into the distance.

But it was Charlotte who first saw the dot on the horizon. "There it is, Chrissy! That's it!"

The dot grew larger and larger to become, finally, a huge ocean liner like the one they were on. Silently, dreamily, they watched the ship approach and then sail majestically by, becoming smaller and smaller until

once again it was only a dot on the far edge of the ocean.

Christene stopped looking once it was clear that all they were seeing was an occasional fleck of foam that the wind stirred up, or a dip in a wave that threw the bright reflection of the September sun back into their eyes. But Charlotte didn't stop. That two ships should somehow find one another in the great, endless Pacific Ocean seemed unbelievable to her. That she should see it happen was still more so. Even after Christene said, "Charlie, you're wasting your time. It's gone," Charlotte kept right on staring and staring.

"Were you thinking the same thing I was?" Christene said. "That if it were still March, it might be us on that other ship going back to America instead of on this one going to China?" A strand of her thick golden hair blew across her lips, and she quickly brushed it away. Her eyes were bright blue and intent on Charlotte.

Despite a carpet of freckles across her nose, everyone said Christene would be a beauty when she grew up, but no one had ever said that about Charlotte. All Charlotte remembered was her mother telling her father that she would have to see an orthodontist on their next home leave when she would be thirteen. Would seeing an orthodontist make her more beautiful? It was never mentioned.

Charlotte didn't reply to Christene's question and pretended to be busy watching the churning white water in the wake of their ship.

"Well, were you, Charlie?" Christene asked again impatiently.

"No," Charlotte said. But she was lying. Of course she'd been thinking it. How could she *not* think it, or wonder how anything they'd dreamed of for so long could be over so suddenly? Their home leave in America had been like Christmas, gone in a minute. But she preferred not to think about it, or talk about it either.

Hair blew across Christene's lips again, and this time she took the strand in her fingers and chewed on it thoughtfully.

"Well, if we were on that ship, we probably wouldn't be us. We'd be someone else, I suppose. Did you ever think, Charlie, that if Daddy hadn't gone to America and met Mother just when she'd quarrelled with that doctor she was engaged to, they might never have married? We might never have been born at all, or if we had, Mother and Daddy would be married to other people and we'd be only half us, and probably quite different."

"No, I'd still be me," said Charlotte firmly. "No matter what!"

"Don't be stupid, Charlie. Of course you wouldn't. Things don't work out that way. It has to do with biology. You'll see after you've had The Talk with Mother." Christene's face took on the important, superior look it always wore when she mentioned "things" she was privileged to know because she was older. It was a look that always made Charlotte furious.

"I don't care what it has to do with," she burst out. "I don't care about The Talk either. It won't change my mind at all."

"All right then, suppose Mother had been an—an Eskimo, or Daddy a Chinese—bandit." Christene paused to see what kind of effect this was having on Charlotte. "Do you think you'd still be the same you?"

"Yes!"

"You're not making sense, Charlie," Christene said coolly.

"I am. I am, too!" Charlotte said, her voice rising. She knew very well she *wasn't* making sense, but Christene was confusing her. Anyway, no one ever made sense when she was having a fight. And from nowhere, suddenly, like most of their fights, that's what this had become.

"Well, I don't know why you're so anxious to be you, anyway," Christene whipped back. "I should think you'd like to have been born someone else who wasn't so skinny and didn't need to have her front teeth pushed back. And someone who"—Christene stopped as if to think of the very worst thing she could possibly say—"didn't have Cousin Philip call her a 'funny little thing'!"

Cousin Philip was the handsome young bachelor cousin of their father's whom Charlotte idolized, so Christene *had* successfully thought of the very worst thing she could say.

Outraged, Charlotte flung back, "You made that up. He never said it!"

"Oh yes, he did! And if you don't believe me, you can ask him when he comes to China next year."

The only argument Charlotte had left was to say in a louder voice exactly what she'd said before. "He never said it!"

"Oh yes, he did!"

"No, he didn't!"

"Did!"

"Didn't!" screamed Charlotte, rushing on before Christene could say anything else. "And anyway—I don't care! I like being skinny. I like my teeth, and nobody will ever put jackets on them. You can't make me say I want to be someone else. I like being me, and I'm going to be me forever. So there!" Charlotte ended with a choking sob.

"Bravo!" a strange voice said.

Surprised, and horrified because they'd been caught fighting, Charlotte whirled around. She and Christene had been much too busy watching the ship pass and then quarrelling with each other to notice the young woman who had joined them on the upper deck, watching the other ship just as they'd been doing.

"Bravo!" the young woman said again, smiling.

And Charlotte, in spite of herself, found herself smiling back through tearful eyes at, of all people, Miss Dumpymouse! That wasn't her real name, of course. It was one Charlotte and Christene had invented for her along with other names they'd made up to fit different strangers aboard ship. Charlotte had thought this one clever and hilariously funny at the time.

"Excuse me for eavesdropping," the young woman said, "but I think it's delightful that you like being the person you are. It's really a wonderful thing to be so definite about oneself." Her eyes were a startling clear blue, very wide and very kind, looking at Charlotte. Suddenly, though the young woman wasn't Charlotte's idea of pretty, she began thinking that "Dumpymouse" wasn't such a clever name after all.

"You're sisters, aren't you?" the young woman added quickly.

Charlotte nodded, smiling shyly, although Christene only stared.

"Are there just the two of you in your family?"

"No, there's Jamey," Charlotte said eagerly. "He's our baby brother. He's in the nursery now."

All at once, talking about it, Charlotte had a wonderful, warm feeling about having a little brother aged three and a half in the ship's nursery. She had a sudden vision of Jamey whirling happily around as she pushed him on the miniature merry-go-round during one of her frequent visits to the nursery. She felt very important playing with her brother in front of the nurse in the starched white uniform, and the nursery smell of Johnson's baby powder and wet diapers was familiar and strangely comforting. Charlotte loved to go to the ship's nursery and would have gone right on telling about it if she'd been asked.

"I'm going to be teaching at the American school in Shanghai," the young woman blurted out. "Will you be going there?"

"No, we're going to Tientsin," said Charlotte.

"Oh, I'm so sorry. I've seen you two girls with your mother and father playing cards together in the game room in the evening—"

"Fish!" Charlotte burst in joyfully, her fight with Christene now forgotten.

"Yes, of course, fish! And hearts, too, I suppose. Anyway, I think that—" But whatever the young woman thought was never said, because just then the steward appeared on deck ringing the chimes that announced the children's midday meal.

"It's time for tiffin," Christene said abruptly. Then she turned away, rudely Charlotte thought, and ran toward the steps.

Charlotte dashed after her, remembering only after she reached the top of the steps that she, too, had rudely run off without a word. Turning, she saw the young woman smile and wave to her. Charlotte smiled and waved back and, feeling better, tore down the steps after Christene.

"Chris, you said we'd play flops before tiffin," she called after her sister. Flops was a game they'd invented where they flopped onto the huge down pillows of the biggest couch in the ship's lounge so that the air rushed up between their legs and made a ridiculous flub-ub-ub-ub sound, like air gushing from a released balloon. The object of the game was to see who could make the loudest noises.

"I don't feel like it," Christene said curtly, marching

quickly ahead of Charlotte all the way to the children's dining room. Christene, at twelve, was old enough to eat with her mother and father if she wanted to, but she still chose the children's dining room. Charlotte couldn't understand it, but was glad all the same.

Today, though, Christene didn't speak to Charlotte all through their noonday meal, nor did she have anything to do with her the rest of the day. That night, they undressed silently in the cabin they shared. Then Charlotte lay in her bed in the dark, waiting for Christene to say good night. Christene, being the older, always got to do everything first, things like saying good night. It was understood. Charlotte had never argued with it. But that night Charlotte waited and waited, and Christene never said it. She was still awake, though. Charlotte could tell.

Then finally she couldn't bear it any longer. "Good night, Chrissy."

Christene still didn't speak, but after a while, she said quietly, "I'm sorry about what I said today, Charlie. I mean about Cousin Philip and the rest of it."

"It's all right, Chrissy, really it is," Charlotte said. "Anyway, I was being silly, wasn't I?"

"No, you weren't really."

"Chrissy, that girl Doris who lived in our building in Los Angeles, she said we were odd because we lived in China. Are we?"

"She said that to me, too. She teased me about my baby dresses. But we're not odd. We're not, Charlie! It makes things different to live in China. But we're the same us, the same family, no matter where we live. And it's not odd!"

"That's what I meant today!" Charlotte sighed happily. "That I don't want to be someone else just because Doris says we're odd. I want us to be us."

"We are us," said Christene, and a happy, relieved silence filled the ship's cabin. Then, "Charlie?"

"Yes?"

"You didn't tell Mother and Daddy I made you cry today, did you?"

"No."

"Did you tell Mother I said anything about The Talk?"

"No, I didn't."

"Charlie?"

"What?"

"We'll play flops tomorrow."

"Ten?" asked Charlotte.

"Fifty!"

"A hundred?"

"A thousand!"

"One million flops?"

"At least," said Christene, yawning. " 'Night, Charlie."

" 'Night, Chrissy."

The ship rolled slowly from side to side—like a giant cradle, Charlotte thought sleepily. She lay listening to the walls of their cabin go creak on one side, then creak on the other, and in a few moments she was sound asleep.

TWO

"CHRIS?" Charlotte sat upright in bed. "Chrissy?"

From Christene's bed came a sleepy grunt.

"Are you awake, Chrissy?"

"No!"

"Oh," Charlotte said, and dropped back down on her pillow. Sighing impatiently, she pulled her blanket up under her chin and lay staring first at her own old tortoiseshell comb and brush off in one corner of the pink-curtained dressing table across the room, then at Christene's new pink cloisonné dresser set, which stretched imposingly across practically the whole dresser top.

Christene and Charlotte were no longer in the cabin they had shared aboard ship. The sun just beginning to light the day outside the window was a September sun, but it was a year older, and Charlotte and Christene were a year older, too—Charlotte, just turned eleven, and Christene, thirteen. They were in their own room now, in their own house in Tientsin, which had, in the past year, become their home. Charlotte rarely thought about the homes they had had before this one.

Though Jamey had his own room with his bed and playthings, directly next to Mr. and Mrs. Barrett, Charlotte and Christene shared a bedroom and another room that they used as a playroom. It had always been that way. Charlotte couldn't imagine what it would be like not to have Christene in the bed next to hers. Her world had always held Christene in it. But it was not the other way around. What would it be like for Christene if I had never been? Charlotte wondered. Would it have been better?

Outside the house, beyond their quiet street, the city stirred and readied itself for the day. The cries and noises of the street vendors already broke through the early morning—the sharp clanging of iron plates jerked upward that was the special sound of the sharpener of scissors and knives, and the clop-clop of pellets striking a gong that announced the arrival of the man who mended broken porcelain. This pattern of sound was interrupted from time to time by the cries of men peddling food, in long, drawn-out wails or short, sharp calls almost like the bark of a dog. Already, early-rising businessmen and rickshaw coolies were sucking almond-flavored congee of ground rice and sugar from bowls, or drawing small meat dumplings or hot steaming noodles into their mouths with chopsticks.

When the sharp, biting Gobi desert winds blew, these hot foods, particularly the noodles, looked to the Barrett children more delicious and desirable than anything in the world. Still, none of them had even tasted a noodle or a bao chiao-tze or a candied crabapple on a stick or a dried apricot or anything purchased from a street vendor. It was not allowed. There might be germs. You could get cholera—and die! The children knew these words so well they were almost like a chant, and yet they continued to be told and told.

The big two-story Western-style house of red brick where the Barretts lived was stirring, too, making the small morning house sounds that marked the beginning of its own day. The servants were already at work, and the sounds they made drifted up to Charlotte and Christene's room. Although Liu, the head servant, padded softly and silently across the polished oak floors and thick Chinese rugs, Charlotte could hear the bamboo rod of his feather duster clicking against the porcelain vases in the living room and against the heavy rosewood carving of the tea tables. Below her window, Coolie's broom swished away coal dust spilled by the men delivering coal to the furnace room. And in the kitchen, a stove shovel scraped, a lid crashed, as Dossafoo fired up the huge iron stove—the black beast Charlotte called it—for the children's oatmeal, Mr. Barrett's egg, and the morning's baking.

Charlotte had known these sounds all her life. She both heard them and didn't hear them. They were familiar, comfortable sounds, but they were background sounds, like the music that went with a motion picture. She didn't stop to think about them or let them interfere with her thoughts.

"Chrissy?"

Christene still refused to answer, though she must

have been at least half awake by then. Well, in time she would have to wake up. Amah Cho Mei, who was now moving softly about in their playroom next door, getting ready the clothes they had chosen for the opening of school, would come to their beds and say, "Missy Chrissy, Missy Charlie, time get up now." But she wasn't there yet, and Christene seemed determined not to open her eyes until she was.

Charlotte groaned softly and slid out from under her bed covers. Amah would be upset at finding her gone. "Mommy say all time must have ten hours sleep!" Mrs. Barrett had lectured about this once, and for Amah Cho Mei it meant ten whole hours, right down to the second. Discovering Charlotte out of bed, she would threaten to tell Mother. But she wouldn't do it. She never reported the children's crimes, no matter how terrible.

Not bothering to put on the embroidered satin slippers by her bed, Charlotte tiptoed out of the room and down the hall past the playroom to Jamey's room. Jamey didn't look at all worried about Amah Cho Mei's opinions on sleep. He was out of bed and had already built a huge wall using the complete set of his blocks. Now, still in his green-and-white-striped pajamas, he was on his hands and knees rolling his battered wooden train around the edge of the rug.

"Poot! Poot! Poot!"

Charlotte entered his room and closed the door softly behind her. Avoiding the oncoming train, she dropped down on Jamey's bed and drew her feet up under her.

"I came to tell you you don't have to be scared about today, Jamey."

"I'm not scared," said Jamey.

"Not the least bit?"

"No," Jamey said. "Poot! Poot! Poot!" Around the rug went the train.

Charlotte had come in prepared to be big sisterly and reassuring, and now there was nothing to be reassuring about. She envied Jamey's indifference to his first day in kindergarten, but it was disappointing to have come in for nothing.

Still, if she wasn't able to offer sympathy, she could at least offer advice. "Jamey, you remember what I told you yesterday—about being excused from class?"

"I raise my hand and ask?" Jamey stopped rolling his train for a moment to demonstrate raising his hand.

"Yes, but that's not all," said Charlotte. "Do you remember what else?"

"No," Jamey said.

"It's about what you *say*, Jamey. You just say, 'I need to be excused.' You don't tell teacher *why!*"

"What if she asks me?" said Jamey.

"She won't," replied Charlotte firmly.

"Even to tell Mommy?"

"No! Jamey, teacher isn't Amah. She doesn't report things like—like *that* to Mother. School is different. School is growing up."

"Oh," said Jamey.

"You're sure you're not the least bit scared?" Charlotte asked hopefully.

"No," said Jamey, and began to roll his train again.

Charlotte decided she might as well leave. There was no further reason to stay and watch Jamey crawl around and around on the rug with his train. It was a pointless game, but boys often played strange and pointless games, she was discovering. And they made strange, outlandish noises. Charlotte was sure she loved Jamey, but she often wondered why her parents, particularly her father, had been so desperately happy about his arrival. Had they been so happy when she, Charlotte, was born?

When Charlotte returned to the bedroom, Christene was on her back with her hands under her head, staring out the window. Charlotte started to flop down on Christene's bed, but then remembered that Christene didn't like it, so she went and flopped on her own.

"Are you awake, Chris?"

"Of course I'm awake—now!" Christene said.

Charlotte overlooked Christene's tone of voice. "Oh, Chrissy, I had the most exciting idea last night. You've got to help me. I couldn't do it alone. It's about Jamey's birthday!"

There was a long pause.

"Well?" said Charlotte.

"Well what?"

"Aren't you going to ask me what it is?"

"Why should I? You're going to tell me anyway, so just go ahead," Christene said.

"It's a surprise for his party, Chrissy!" announced Charlotte.

"Charlie, you know that his party's already been planned."

"All of it?"

"Yes. *And* he's going to have bao chiao-tzes and chocolate cake"—Christene paused impressively—"*with* chopsticks!"

"Chopsticks?" Charlotte squealed. The boiled dough-covered meat dumplings called bao chiao-tzes and chocolate cake were always served at Barrett birthday parties because it was what the children invariably wanted. But chopsticks instead of forks? Neither Christene nor Charlotte had ever been allowed chopsticks at their parties! "For the chocolate cake, too? Who ever heard of eating chocolate cake with chopsticks?"

"Nobody," said Christene. "But it's what Jamey wants, and Mother is going to allow it."

"Is he going to have the Pa Hsi Man, too?" breathed Charlotte, unbelieving. It didn't seem possible that someone in their family could be allowed both chopsticks at the table and the Chinese magician at the very same party.

"Yes," Christene replied. "I don't really see where you're going to be able to have any surprises, Charlie."

"Well—well—" Charlotte stumbled. "When the Pa Hsi Man is finished, I'll put on a tall magician's hat with stars and moons on it like Merlin's, and a big blanket around my shoulders for a cape. Then I'll come out with my present for Jamey under the blanket!"

"That's a lot of silly fuss just to give him a cricket cage. It's not much of a surprise, if you ask me."

Charlotte leaped from her bed and tiptoed dramatically to the door. Having determined that Amah Cho Mei was not on her way, she tiptoed back. "Oh, no, I'm not giving him the cricket cage! This is something else. Chrissy, I'm going to give him a puppy. A *live* one!"

Charlotte dropped down on Christene's bed, certain now that she wouldn't be invited to leave.

"Where are you going to get a puppy?" Christene asked.

"From a Chinese clerk at the grocery store, the compradore! Dossafoo told me about them."

Christene didn't need to ask why Dossafoo had given Charlotte this important piece of information. Charlotte was always hanging around the kitchen, "bothering the servants," as Mrs. Barrett said. "Well, Dossafoo gives me dough from the mixing bowl and talks to me, so he can't mind it too much, can he?" Charlotte always replied. At any rate, though Dossafoo dutifully complained to Mrs. Barrett from time to time about Charlotte's continued presence in the kitchen, nothing much was done about it.

"What kind are they?" asked Christene.

"Dossafoo says there are all kinds—black-and-white ones and brown ones. He says one is black with a white nose."

"Charlie, I don't mean what color are they. I mean what *kind* are they. Are they purebreds or wonks?"

Charlotte shrugged. "I guess I don't know. I never asked."

"Well, are they selling them or giving them away?"

"Oh, they're giving them away," said Charlotte brightly.

"Then they're wonks all right," Christene said matter-of-factly. "They're the only kind anyone *gives* away. And if they are, you'd better forget about your surprise. Daddy's always said if we have a dog, it'll be a purebred."

"Well," said Charlotte, "he's never let *us* have any dog!"

It was true. Though the girls had pleaded for a dog desperately, they'd never been allowed to have one because of quarantine and other complications that went with owning a dog when people traveled between countries.

"But, Chrissy," Charlotte added, "he might let us keep this one if we make it a present to Jamey. He wouldn't make Jamey give up a present, would he? Oh, please, Chris, do it with me. I can't do it if you don't help me. Please!"

Frowning, Christene thought a moment, and then shrugged. "I don't see how it can possibly work, Charlie, but oh well, I guess I'll do it with you."

"Oh, Chrissy!"

"Of course," Christene said, "we can't possibly go to the compradore ourselves to get the puppy. If anyone found out, there'd be a riot. We'll have to choose one sight unseen, and then have someone get it for us."

Charlotte marveled at the way Christene's mind had already gone to work, planning carefully. She herself would have just jumped into it, and the whole thing would have been a disaster before it even started. "Shall we get Liu?" she asked quickly.

"Liu reports everything, Charlie. You know that. We'll have to find someone more trustworthy than Liu, at least trustworthy to *us*. But you'd better get back in bed, Charlie. Amah's coming. We'll talk about it later."

By the time Amah Cho Mei hobbled in on her tiny bound feet, both girls had their eyes tightly shut, pretending sleep. "Missy Chrissy, Missy Charlie, time get up now! Ten hours sleep finish!" Amah was proud and happy making this announcement.

Charlotte didn't want to wait until later to finish making plans with Christene. She wanted to go on talking as they dressed, but Christene grabbed her clothes

from the playroom and went with them to the bathroom, as she'd been doing for several weeks. For as long
as Charlotte could remember, they had dressed and
undressed together. Now Christene dressed and undressed in the privacy of the bathroom.

Did it, Charlotte wondered, have something to do
with The Talk? She'd had that by now, the one their
mother gave. It was strange, though. Charlotte had
once thought that when she'd had The Talk, she and
Christene would hold discussions about it, but they
never had.

Anyway, what difference did it all make? Christene
was in with her on the puppy conspiracy. They would
always do things like this together. Growing up was
something you spoke to Jamey about on his first day of
kindergarten. It had nothing to do with the two of
them.

THREE

TWO afternoons later they were in the den talking over
the arrangements for what Charlotte now called "the
Puppy Plot." Christene was sprawled on the couch, an
open book lying over her stomach, sipping from a tall
glass filled with ice and ginger ale. Charlotte lay on her
stomach on the floor, dunking toast in a cup of hot chocolate. She had made the hot chocolate and toast herself
in the kitchen. She had also made a terrible mess
doing it.

"Dossafoo will be very glad not to have *you* around
for a month," Christene informed Charlotte. "It's a good
thing we had your promise to stay out of the kitchen
for a bribe."

"I don't think I can stand it," said Charlotte, and
flung herself over on her back, so she lay staring at the
ceiling.

"You'd better," Christene said drily.

The bribe had been Christene's idea. She had decided that Dossafoo was the one to be approached about getting the puppy since he had been the one to tell Charlotte about the puppies in the first place. But she felt they ought to offer him something "just to be sure," as she put it.

Charlotte offered him two weeks.

"Missy Charlie stay out one month, Dossafoo can do. Can get puppy," said Dossafoo.

"You'd better promise it," Christene prompted.

So Charlotte did. Beginning the day the puppy arrived in the house, she was to stay out of the kitchen for a month.

"Why didn't we offer Amah a bribe?" Charlotte asked, rolling back onto her stomach.

Christene sucked a piece of ice into her mouth, rolled it around, and then let it slide back into her glass. "Don't be stupid, Charlie. You know we don't have to offer Amah anything."

"I know," said Charlotte. The picture flashed into her mind of Amah Cho Mei upstairs embroidering purple plum blossoms on a pair of silk slippers, and at the same time keeping a watchful eye on Jamey playing in his room. In her white cotton jacket and black trousers, her oiled black hair drawn back into a tight bun on her neck, Amah Cho Mei, like all the other amahs they'd had, would do anything for the children in the family. With Amah, they knew they could get away with whatever they wanted.

Amah Cho Mei had threatened, of course, to tell Mrs. Barrett about the puppy. "No can do. Mommy get very angry." But in the end, grumbling and grousing, she'd agreed to help them.

"Do you really think she'll do it?" Charlotte asked.

"She'll do it," said Christene, and gurgled down the last of her ginger ale. She peered into the empty glass reflectively. "I still say I don't think it's going to work, but"—she shrugged—"this is the plan, I guess. Dossafoo will get the puppy the night before Jamey's party. It will have to be after Jamey has gone to bed so that Amah can sit with the puppy in her room and keep him quiet. Otherwise Liu—"

"The villain!" interrupted Charlotte.

"Oh, Charlie, he's not a villain. For heaven's sake!"

"Yes, he is," Charlotte insisted. "He's the villain of the Puppy Plot. We're the heroines!"

"Oh, for heaven's sake!" Christene repeated.

"The villain Liu," Charlotte said dreamily.

"Charlie, Liu is only—oh well, all right." Christene sighed. "Otherwise the villain Liu will hear him and become suspicious. If we want to see the puppy, we'll take turns and not form a parade each time we go down. Now—"

"The next day we take turns staying with him," Charlotte burst in, "until the party when I go down to Amah's room, put on my Merlin hat and cape, and bring him up. Oh, Chrissy, I can't stand it! I'll die waiting!" Charlotte rolled over on her back again and hugged herself in despair.

"No, you won't," Christene said. "Anyway, if you do, it's all right. I'm sure there will be someone else who'd be glad to bring him up." She picked up the book that was lying on her stomach and began calmly to read.

Charlotte stared at the ceiling and groaned.

"Don't step on the spit!" Charlotte shrieked.

They were walking to school two weeks later, Jamey hopping along the sidewalk from crack to crack, lost in his own private game, and just in time, Charlotte had seen him about to leap on a small, glistening mass that lay in his path.

Jamey sidestepped it neatly. But instead of walking by, he stopped, cleared his throat noisily, and spat. A second shiny mass now lay by the first one, and Jamey leaned over to examine it. "There, I spitted just as good as he did!"

Charlotte was dying to see if Jamey was right, but decided she probably shouldn't. "Jamey, I don't think you ought to do that. Spitting on the street isn't good manners."

"Alfred Wang and I had a spit contest in school yesterday at recess. *He* says it's all right for Chinese to spit anyplace. He says I spit good!"

"You spit *well*, Jamey. Anyway, Alfred doesn't know what he's talking about. I bet his mother and father don't know he's going around saying things like that. It isn't good manners for Chinese or anybody else to spit all over the place. *You* shouldn't do it. Chrissy, don't you think Jamey shouldn't spit on the sidewalk?"

"Oh, honestly! Can't you find anything better to talk about?" Christene's voice was strangely sharp, and Charlotte was surprised to see that her face was flushed.

The broad street they took for most of the way to

school was quiet this time of morning, almost deserted. In a residential section of the city, the street was lined with acacia trees and large brick Western-style houses, which were the homes of Chinese and foreign business-men and their families. Two or three rickshaws and an occasional car passed them as they walked to school, but beyond that, they had had the street almost to themselves. Now someone was coming out through the front gate of the house across the street, a young girl.

Charlotte knew the girl, but not very well. Her name was Moira Evans, and she was with Christene in the eighth grade, though they'd never been friends. This was because Moira was glued to another girl named Polly Willard. She'd never had time for Christene or anyone else. Polly and her family had recently left for America on home leave, and Moira was now busy mak-ing friends with a new girl in the class.

"Trying her out, I suppose," Christene had said indifferently the first day of school.

Beyond Christene's comments, Charlotte didn't know much about Moira, but what she did know, she didn't like much. All the past winter, Moira had worn a navy blue coat with a wide collar of real fur. Chris-tene and Charlotte's coats had real fur collars, too, only theirs were Chinese alley cat, while Moira's was some-thing like lamb or squirrel that came from a real fur store. That a young girl should have a coat trimmed in something other than Chinese alley cat, which was just as warm as any other fur, made her horribly spoiled, Charlotte thought.

But what was even worse in Charlotte's mind was that Moira didn't wear the serviceable tan lisle stockings that she and Christene wore, with knitted wool leggings added when the Gobi winds blew stinging sand against their legs. Instead, Moira wore long white stockings and patent leather pumps all winter, because she rode to school each day in her own private rickshaw with her legs wrapped in a blanket. Charlotte considered it completely disgusting that anyone should have to be pulled the six short blocks to school in a rickshaw, and she understood perfectly why Christene seemed indifferent to the idea of Moira as a friend.

"Christene! Christ-*ee*-eene!" Moira's voice rang musically across the street. "Wait for me. I'm walking today, but I have to say good-bye to Mother. I'll be right over."

To Charlotte's surprise, Christene looked pleased and came to a dead halt. Charlotte decided she might as well come to a halt, too.

"Charlie, you don't have to wait," Christene said carelessly.

"Oh, I don't mind," said Charlotte. "I don't want to walk with her, but I want to walk with you, Chrissy."

"Well, she only asked *me* to wait, not all of us," Christene snapped. "Look, now Jamey's coming back! Oh, Charlie, *please!*"

She's trying to get rid of us—of me! Charlotte thought suddenly. She's trying to get rid of us because of that charming, wonderful Moira!

"Oh, all right," Charlotte said. She tried to sound cheery and ignorant as if she didn't know what it was all about. "I'll run up ahead with Jamey."

As Charlotte started off, Christene called out, "I'll see you at school, Charlie!" It sounded like an apology.

It was the kind of apology, though, that did as much good as having the doctor say, "This won't hurt a bit," as he jabbed the needle into her arm for a typhoid shot. Charlotte would almost have preferred to have Christene say nothing. The words hadn't stopped the feeling she suddenly had in the middle of her stomach, as if someone had struck her there with a cold, hard pebble.

Darting forward, she called to Jamey, "Let's race to the bridge!" Her voice came out strange and breathless, as if she'd already been racing.

The bridge was only a small concrete one crossing a narrow, muddy brown creek that smelled terrible any time except dead winter when it was frozen over. This wasn't surprising. The creek was used by the Chinese who lived along its banks for kitchen purposes, bathroom purposes, all purposes. But Charlotte never questioned any of this. There were creeks like it everywhere in China. She had been born in a house by a creek just like this one. When you came to the bridge, you simply held your breath and hurried across it. That was all.

"It stinks!" Jamey said when they arrived panting on the opposite side of the creek. He looked sideways at Charlotte to see what she'd say about this remark.

"You're right," Charlotte replied blandly.

Jamey looked at her in surprise. "But I'm not supposed to say that!"

"I know," said Charlotte. "But today it's all right."

"Who said so?"

"*I* said so." Charlotte looked back over her shoulder and saw Christene and Moira with their heads together, jabbering at full speed. "It stinks!" Charlotte said. She liked the way it sounded. "It stinks!" she said again.

Jamey grinned. "It stinks! Stinky, stinky, stinks!"
"Yes, it does," said Charlotte.
Satisfied, they marched on to school.

There were many kinds of schools in Tientsin—
Chinese school, British school, French school. The
Barrett children went to the American school. It was in
a large brick building that looked as if it had once been
someone's house. The playground might once have been
a tremendous and beautiful garden with mimosa trees
and peonies, a pond filled with water lilies and black
fantailed fish. Now it was only dust and swings and
monkey bars surrounded by a high gray concrete wall.
Beyond the wall at the end of the playground was the
river.

It was the Hai River, lazy and wide and mud-brown,
and to Charlotte not any different from the Yangtze
River they'd lived near before. But Dossafoo had said
to her, "River in China like sleeping dragon. Very dangerous! Can become angry, like dragon, and swallow
country in flood. Many people no have homes. Many
die!" Dossafoo had been in a flood, he said, but Charlotte
had never seen one. Sometimes she had the feeling she
wouldn't mind being in a flood once just to see what it
was all about, but she hadn't really made up her mind
about it. As Dossafoo said, a flood was a terrible thing.
Perhaps, like a cholera epidemic, it was better only to
hear about it and no more.

In the meantime, it was hard to imagine anything
dangerous about the lazy-looking rivers she had known.
They were simply another kind of Chinese business
street, with tiny sampans on which whole families lived,

crowded up against the muddy banks, and huge cargo-carrying junks sailing imperiously by. Charlotte loved watching the junks pass. Once she and Christene had spent the night on the deck of the launch belonging to the oil company their father worked for. Charlotte had awakened in the middle of the night and seen a junk passing them. With its huge patched sails reaching up into the night, making a magical silhouette against the moonlight, it cut through the river without a sound, completely silent. It was like a beautiful wish, a fantasy, a dream. Charlotte had watched the junk until her eyes ached, and when it was gone and there was only the moonlight left, she was sure she had imagined it, that it *was* a dream.

It was only when the junks were anchored by the riverbanks that she could ever believe they were business ships with ordinary, everyday work to do. "Aiya-hoa! Aiya-hoa!" Standing at the far end of the school playground, the children could hear the Chinese coolies chanting singsong as they strained under the burlap sacks of peanuts and grain they carried off the junks to load onto waiting carts. "Aiya-hoa! Aiya-hoa!" From behind the high gray walls of the school, it was a constant reminder of life on the river.

Still, most of the time, Charlotte never consciously thought about the river. It was simply there. Within the walls of the school playground, the building, school was school. Cities and countrysides flooded, sweating coolies strained under crushing loads, families lived and worked and died crowded together on one tiny sampan, fairy-tale boats sailed down wide rivers, and still you had to go to school.

Charlotte left Jamey off at the monkey bars with his kindergarten friends and trudged up to the room the fifth and sixth grades shared on the second floor of the school building. She was in no hurry to get there, but there was no point in standing around outside by herself. Ordinarily she waited with Christene until the bell rang, but today she had the feeling that it would be better for her to disappear. She went up the stairs disgusted with Christene, hating Moira Evans. Moira had even managed, at least for the moment, to dull Charlotte's excitement over the Puppy Plot.

"Stink!" said Charlotte to herself. She was surprised at how little guilt she felt in saying it. In fact, it was amazingly pleasant. It was like a secret weapon she could use to comfort herself while not actually hurting anyone. The thought came to her that she should remember to use it again.

The satisfaction of saying a word forbidden in her family didn't last long, however, and after Charlotte had arranged her books neatly in her desk drawer, she sank into her seat in a discouraged heap. Besides the immediate problem of Moira, school was a huge disappointment this year, and it didn't look as if anything was ever going to change. The fifth and sixth grades had a substitute teacher whom they feared they might have forever.

"Wasn't the school lucky to find Mrs. Cornwall," Mrs. Barrett had said when it was announced that Mrs. Baker, the scheduled teacher, was to have a baby just before school opened in September. "What would they have done without her?"

Lots of things, Charlotte told herself. She would

have gotten through the sixth grade, for one thing. Mrs. Cornwall was the slowest person she'd ever met in her life. You could fall asleep waiting while she erased the blackboard, and on top of that, she made the class go over everything about fifty times. Did Mrs. Cornwall expect them to memorize the whole sixth grade? In Charlotte's opinion, if the school wasn't lucky enough to find *another* teacher, they'd all have to repeat the sixth grade because they'd never get past Chapter I of anything.

Another disappointment about school was one Charlotte had had all along and should have grown used to, although she never quite did. It was that she'd never had a good friend from school, and this year, once again, there wasn't a single likely prospect in the class. Her classmates were all the same ones she'd had last year. It was unusual for a class in a foreign school in China not to have some old members leave and some new ones come in each year, but somehow the sixth grade had managed it. Ignoring the fifth grade because they weren't the ones who mattered, Charlotte sat disconsolately jabbing black pencil holes in her brand-new Pink Pearl eraser as the rest of the sixth grade drifted into the room.

First came the two Chinese students in her class—Anna Chung in bobbed hair and slender Chinese-style blue cotton gown, and her brother William in an ill-fitting Western-style suit. They always arrived at exactly three minutes before the bell rang. They never came any earlier or any later, and Charlotte had rarely seen either one smile. They somehow managed to look as if they had been chased all the way to school.

As soon as the bell rang, two boys came in—Barry Dameron and Horace Buttrick, who was called Skinny. Barry was one of the "Army brats," a name given to children of members of the United States Army, who came to school in a mule-drawn wagon. Charlotte didn't think "brat" was a good term for Barry, though. He had freckles and sandy hair and wasn't bad, for a boy. When school had first started, he had swung with her at recess until two droopy girls from the seventh grade, who let it be known they thought Barry was "cute," started singing stupid things like:

"Charlotte and Barry in a tree,
Kay-I-Ess-Ess-I-En-Gee;
First comes love, then comes marriage,
Then comes Charlotte with a baby carriage."

After that, Barry didn't swing with Charlotte anymore. It was too bad, Charlotte thought. He'd been a good person to swing with.

Barry's best friend was Skinny Buttrick, whose parents were missionaries. Charlotte envied him because he lived right in Chinese City. Of course, all of Tientsin was a Chinese city, but *real* Chinese City was considered to be the part that lay beyond the big brick and stone houses and buildings, broad streets, and foreign stores. Though she knew where it was, Charlotte had never been there, but Skinny told everyone about the narrow streets lined with houses whose tiled roofs curled up at the corners, and rows of small, dimly lit shops, open at the front so you could look in and see the sticks of candied crabapples, cooked ducks that looked as if they had been dipped in bright red lacquer, and glass-topped counters filled with hundreds of exciting things. Sometimes Skinny would bring some of these things to school—painted fans, miniature glass animals, slates with tiny round felt erasers that Chinese children used in their schools, firecrackers, and sticks of sesame candy. Charlotte had seen many houses and shops like the ones Skinny talked about, but never all clustered together the way Skinny described them. It sounded wonderful to her, and she determined that someday she would go see it for herself.

It wasn't until the final bell that the last two members of the sixth grade strolled in—Walter Francis and Eddy Schmidt. Walter was just another boy in Charlotte's mind. The only thing that distinguished him was an old gray sweater with a black Indian design on it that he had worn all through fifth grade and now seemed destined to wear all through sixth. About all he accomplished beyond that was to follow Eddy Schmidt around and get into trouble with him.

Eddy sat in the desk behind Charlotte. He had been in the fifth grade two years and the fourth grade two years before that. He was much too big for his desk, and when he leaned on his desk top, he seemed to breathe right down Charlotte's neck. Charlotte wished she could turn around and ask Eddy to sit up and breathe someplace else, but Eddy was the kind of boy that if you asked him *not* to do something, he'd keep on doing it, only with added attractions. It was safer to keep still.

And that was the whole sixth grade—Charlotte and Anna and five boys. Charlotte sighed as Eddy flopped down in his desk so hard it made *her* desk shake. Mrs.

Cornwall hadn't yet arrived, and a general racket started up in the classroom. Charlotte felt a whap on her arm with a ruler.

"Hey," Eddy shouted right by Charlotte's ear. "I've got a new one! Wanna hear it?" Without waiting for any sign from Charlotte, Eddy said something in Chinese, then thrust one leg out next to Charlotte, slapping it and guffawing loudly.

Charlotte didn't turn around. She couldn't bear the sight of Eddy's face up so close that she could see the fuzz growing on his chin and upper lip. But the back of Charlotte's head didn't seem to deter Eddy.

"Hey! Wanna hear what it means?"

Eddy Schmidt was the self-appointed central agency for bringing to the school choice Chinese insults and their translations. Lots of times little groups of boys huddled around Eddy in the playground, roaring with laughter. It often sounded like fake laughter to Charlotte. The boys laughed, she decided, because no boy would admit to any other boy that he really didn't understand what Eddy was talking about. Eddy usually reserved his information for the boys, except when he could corner Charlotte. She wasn't above having an interest in learning some colorful Chinese insults, but she wasn't interested in learning anything from Eddy Schmidt, especially not today.

"No," Charlotte hissed through her teeth, staring rigidly down at her desk top.

Eddy would probably have translated the insult anyway, except at that moment the entire class became suddenly hushed. It was only because Charlotte had her gaze so firmly fastened to her desk that she hadn't seen anyone walk in.

"Good morning, everyone!"

Surprised, Charlotte looked up and saw a young woman standing in front of the teacher's desk, leaning against it, her arms folded in front of her.

"I'm sorry I'm so late," she continued, "but my being here is very sudden and very unexpected, and I had to go over some things with Mrs. Cornwall before I came in this morning. In any event, my name is Miss Bell. I've just come from Shanghai, and I'll be teaching the fifth and sixth grades for the rest of this year. But now, before we get into the schoolwork for today, I'd like to know something about all of you. We'll start at the far corner of the room. Just tell me your full name, please, and then what you prefer to be called." Smiling, the new teacher nodded in Charlotte's direction.

Charlotte blurted out, "My name is Charlotte Barrett, and I like to be called Charlie. And you're Miss Dump—" Charlotte stumbled, feeling herself blush furiously. "I mean, you're the lady who talked to us on the ship coming back from America a year ago!"

Miss Bell peered at Charlotte more closely and then laughed. "Why, you're right! What a lovely surprise! So you're going to be in my class after all."

Charlotte forgot her embarrassment at once and smiled shyly back at her new teacher.

"Now," Miss Bell continued, "would the gentleman behind you like to give me his name?"

Eddy must have been so startled at being called a gentleman that it took him some time to get himself and his name together.

Suddenly the world, and the sixth grade in particular, took on a whole new direction for Charlotte. No more Mrs. Cornwall! The sixth grade was going to have a bright, sparkling new teacher named Miss Bell. Charlotte wondered how she and Christene had ever invented the name "Dumpymouse." As for Christene, well, by Monday Moira might decide to ride to school as she always did, and that would be the end of that. And tonight there would be a new puppy in their home!

It was amazing, but in exactly two minutes, everything had changed. Charlotte carefully laid her Pink Pearl eraser in her desk and, for no reason at all, turned and smiled sweetly at Eddy Schmidt.

FOUR

THAT afternoon, Christene stayed late to go to the school library with Moira. Since Amah always came for Jamey when kindergarten ended at noon, Charlotte went home alone. She dawdled most of the way because Christene had said that she and Moira would be riding home together in Moira's rickshaw. Charlotte told herself that it ought to be a funny sight, and she shouldn't miss seeing it. But the more she thought about it, the less funny it seemed, and the less she liked the idea of hanging around someplace spying on her own sister. After dragging her feet slowly past the place where Jamey had spit that morning (the spit was still there she noticed), she concluded the whole thing wasn't worth it and trudged on home.

Anyway, across the street from their house, in the huge empty field that was big enough to hold at least ten houses, something far more interesting than Christene and Moira in a rickshaw was taking place. The Chinese family named Yueh who lived in the corner house directly across from the Barretts was staging a funeral feast. That morning as they left for school, Charlotte, Christene, and Jamey had seen the workmen and servants setting up the tables for it, and now it was in full swing.

Hypnotized by the enormousness of the affair, Charlotte stood in front of their garden gate watching the crowds of Chinese, hundreds of them, milling around, talking, laughing, sucking up hot food from bowls. There were steaming cauldrons of food on dozens of serving tables, and the smell of hot oil and soy sauce and cooked meat was heavy in the September afternoon. Tonight, after dinner, the smell of the food, which would last for the three days and nights of the feast, might make Charlotte feel ill. But this afternoon it made her feel as if she were starving.

She didn't cross the street because she was frightened to go, and besides, she would be skinned alive by her parents if they found out about it. But if it hadn't been for those two things, she *could* have gone, because you didn't need an invitation. The people at the feast were almost all strangers, stuffing themselves courtesy of the Yueh relatives who, by offering this magnificent feast to the poor as a bribe to the gods, believed they were assuring a smooth passage into heaven for Great-great-grandfather Yueh, who had just died.

Charlotte didn't know Great-great-grandfather Yueh any more than all the people enjoying his fine funeral feast. She only knew that there was such a person because Dossafoo had told her he had died. A very old man named Mr. Yueh had lived and now had died in the house across the street, and Charlotte had never even seen him. Except for the gatekeeper who guarded the tall iron gates, she rarely saw anyone from the Yueh mansion.

What would it be like, she wondered, to be a part of one of these great, rich Chinese families who spun out their secret lives in big gray houses, separated from the street by high walls studded forbiddingly with broken glass, and a tall iron gate guarded by a gate-keeper? From time to time someone within these mysterious fortresses would die. Then a long funeral procession would form outside the gates, with white-robed professional mourners and men waving rods of feathery make-believe tears. Or someone would be married, and a magnificent brightly colored wedding procession, led by noisy musicians, would line up to escort the sedan chair of a bride to her new home. These things were all that Charlotte saw or knew about the lives of the Yueh family that lived across the street from her.

Suddenly, as she watched the crowd at the funeral feast, a large puff of black smoke billowed up at the far end of the field. A hush fell on the crowd for a moment, and then a murmur of approval flowed through it as the smoke rose into the air. They were burning mock paper money and mock paper food and paper figures of horses and servants that would all go with Great-great-grandfather Yueh to make his life more comfortable in heaven.

The Chinese policeman on the street corner turned to Charlotte, smiling his approval of what had just happened. Charlotte smiled back, and then, remembering the exciting news about Miss Bell she had yet to report to her mother, she banged open the garden gate, stomped up the stairs, and rang the doorbell impatiently until Liu came to let her in. Then she tore into the hall yelling, "Mother, guess what!"

Liu scowled at her. "Shhh, Missy Charlie. Mother in living room with guest."

"Oh?" said Charlotte, dumping her books on the hall chair. "Who?"

"Missy Shaw," Liu replied.

Charlotte turned right around and headed back toward the front door. If seeing her mother meant seeing Mrs. Shaw, Charlotte preferred not to see her mother. She intended to go back outside and come through the kitchen door where she could sneak up the back stairs to the playroom. But she was too late. Her mother had already heard her.

"We're in the living room, Charlie. There's someone here who wants to see you, dear." Mrs. Barrett sang it out in a silvery party-time voice that was very put on because she knew how Charlotte felt about Mrs. Shaw.

With a resigned shrug, Charlotte turned and headed once more for the door to the living room.

"It's Aunty Mabel, dear," Mrs. Barrett announced gaily as Charlotte entered.

Mrs. Shaw wasn't really Aunty Mabel at all. She wasn't Aunty anything, but had always insisted that the Barrett children call her that because they'd known each other for years and years. They were all supposed to feel sorry for Aunty Mabel because she had no children of her own, but Charlotte didn't. She didn't feel anything about it at all.

46

Charlotte knew exactly what Aunty Mabel would do when she walked into the room, and Aunty Mabel did it. She held out her arms and said, "Come, let Aunty Mabel give little Charlotte a big hug and kiss!"

This kind of thing was unpleasant enough when you were small and round and younger than Jamey, but now "little Charlotte" was long and string beany, and when she sat on Aunty Mabel's lap, her legs hung way down to the floor. Still, her mother gave her a firm look, and she had to trail over and allow herself to be clutched down onto Aunty Mabel's waiting lap.

"Now, what was it you wanted to say, dear? Was it something that happened in school today?" Mrs. Barrett gave Charlotte an encouraging smile.

"No, it really wasn't anything," said Charlotte stiffly. This was a lie. She was bursting to tell her mother about Miss Bell, but how could you carry on a dignified conversation when you were dangling off somebody's lap? Surely her mother could see that she felt ridiculous. Or did her mother feel sorrier for Aunty Mabel than for her own children? Charlotte glared across the room.

Mrs. Barrett returned the glare with a limp smile. "Oh yes," she said vaguely. "Well then, Charlie dear, give Aunty Mabel another kiss, then run along upstairs and see how Jamey is."

Running upstairs to see how Jamey was, was a family method of getting rid of Charlotte and Christene in an embarrassing situation. This time Charlotte was grateful, and she could even tolerate the suggestion of another kiss as long as it meant escape. She allowed Aunty Mabel to plant a kiss on her rigidly extended cheek, then raced for the stairs.

"Charlie," her mother called after her, "where's Chris? Didn't she come home with you?"

Charlotte paused briefly at the foot of the stairs. "She stayed at school with—with that Moira Evans."

"Oh?" said Mrs. Barrett. It was an important sounding "oh." Charlotte would like to have asked her mother what it meant, but she didn't want to end up back on Aunty Mabel's lap, so she proceeded up the stairs, two at a time.

"Charlie?"

Charlotte stopped and leaned over the banister.

"Dear, I forgot to tell you, the funnies came today," said Mrs. Barrett.

"The funnies?" Charlotte shrieked, and nearly came tumbling back down the stairs. "Where are they? Mother, you didn't let Jamey have them!"

"No, of course I didn't let Jamey have them," said Mrs. Barrett calmly. "They're in your bedroom, hidden under Christene's bed. But I think, dear—"

Charlotte didn't wait to hear what her mother thought, and promptly disappeared from view.

The day the six-month collection of Sunday funnies arrived from their Grandmother Barrett in the United States was a tremendous event in the lives of Christene and Charlotte. It was, in a way, second only to Christmas. The girls always sorted them together, hoarding in a special pile "Tarzan of the Apes," and Jamey wasn't allowed to touch them until the girls were entirely through with them.

Charlotte pulled the bundle from under Christene's bed, but then helpless and frustrated, she only sat and looked at it. She and her sister had always done this together. Christene had deserted her for Moira this afternoon, but to dig into the funnies alone was a traitorous act of monumental proportions. And Christene had promised she'd be back within the hour, hadn't she? Charlotte shoved the bundle back under the bed without even untying the cord.

Christene didn't come back within the hour. She didn't even come back within two hours. Shortly before six o'clock, a note from Moira arrived via the Evans' coolie, asking if Christene could stay at their house for dinner. It was eight o'clock before Christene arrived home, just as Jamey was being put to bed. She burst into their bedroom where Charlotte lay on her stomach on the floor reading *Little Women*. There wasn't a newspaper in sight.

"Where are they? Daddy said the funnies had come. Where are they?" Christene's look seemed to accuse Charlotte of already having sorted them, read them, and burned them.

Charlotte reached out and pulled the bundle from under the bed once more. "Here. I didn't touch them, Chrissy."

Embarrassed, Christene dropped to her knees before the bundle of funny papers. "You didn't have to wait for me, Charlie."

"I know," said Charlotte, "but I did anyway. Chrissy, did you forget about the puppy's coming tonight?" That was the thing that was hurting Charlotte the most—that Christene could have forgotten the Puppy Plot, that she didn't really care about it.

Christene began pulling the papers apart. "Of course not, silly! Why do you think I got home exactly at eight? Moira wanted me to stay another hour, but I told her I couldn't."

She sounded so matter-of-fact that any ideas Charlotte had about a further discussion of Moira were forgotten. But Charlotte didn't really feel satisfied until later that evening. Mr. and Mrs. Barrett were in the den, safely engrossed in their reading. Dossafoo had come upstairs secretly to announce the arrival of the puppy, and Charlotte had sneaked down behind him to see it safely asleep on Amah Cho Mei's lap in her room.

Now she sat on the top step of the second landing of the stairway, waiting for Christene to come back from her turn at seeing him. This was Charlotte's favorite place in the house. She used it for spying on her parents' cocktail parties, for stealing the first look at the Christmas tree just after all the candles had been lit, for simply sitting and thinking. Tonight she had to hug her knees to keep from exploding over the thought that there was a real live puppy in their house. Somehow, even though she'd just seen him, it seemed an impossible thing to believe.

It couldn't have been more than ten minutes, but Charlotte had gone to look at the clock in their room at least four times before Christene came creeping stealthily up the stairs. Her face was flushed, her eyes dancing as she dropped down beside Charlotte.

"Oh, Charlie," she whispered, "he's adorable! He's the cutest, most wonderful thing I've ever seen. I'm glad you thought of doing this, Charlie. I really am!"

They sat whispering on the stairs until at last Mr. Barrett called out from the den, "What in blazes is going on up there? Don't you two think you ought to be in bed?"

Giggling, the girls ran to their room.

They were conspirators, Christene and Charlotte. They were roommates. They were friends. Moira Evans could have Christene at school all she wanted, and sometimes after school, too. But at home, Christene belonged to Charlotte.

FIVE

CHARLOTTE, using great restraint, was ready for Jamey's party only an hour ahead of time. Anything earlier than that, she felt (and Christene informed her) might look suspicious, especially since the year before she and Christene had fought against attending his party.

"Well," Charlotte said, running the comb through her hair one last time, "it's a good thing I am dressed because somebody has to stay with the puppy while Amah gets Jamey ready."

"You'd better be careful," Christene said.

"Oh, I will be! Chrissy, did I tell you I'm going to call him Maximilian, Max for short?"

Christene made a wry face. "Charlie, *you* are not going to call him anything. He's going to be *Jamey's* dog."

"Oh, that's right," said Charlotte vaguely, and left for the basement.

With the villain Liu in the kitchen helping Dossafoo, Charlotte had no difficulty sneaking down to the basement, where she spent fifty marvelous minutes playing with the puppy Maximilian, practicing wearing her cape and hiding him under it. All she could think was that in only an hour, that unbelievably soft black ball of wool with the white nose would be a member of the Barrett family, not hiding out like a criminal in the basement.

When Amah Cho Mei finally arrived announcing that everyone was now ready for the party, Charlotte flew upstairs. She was surprised to find not only her mother, Christene, and Jamey in the living room, but her father as well, stretched out in a chair, with Jamey sprawled on the arm beside him.

"Daddy! What are you doing here?" Charlotte cried.

"Well, that's a warm welcome," said Mr. Barrett drily. "I'm attending Jamey's party. What's wrong with that?"

"You—you never came to *our* parties!" Charlotte stumbled on the words.

Mr. Barrett laughed. "I happen to share Jamey's feelings about the Pa Hsi Man. And what do you think about him, Jamey?"

"Ding hao, Daddy!" Jamey said.

"That's my boy!" Mr. Barrett put his arm around Jamey and pulled him onto his lap. There Jamey lay, giggling. " 'Very good' is exactly how I feel about him, too. So, Missy Charlie, I decided to take the afternoon off and see the Pa Hsi Man with Jamey."

"But, Daddy—" Charlotte began, intending to ask why he had never done this before. But the doorbell rang, and Jamey dragged Mr. Barrett into the hall to watch Liu usher in the guests and their mothers. As the visitors entered, the eerie, mournful wail of funeral horns drifted in with them from the feast still going on across the street.

Charlotte was curious to see what Jamey's spitting friend, Alfred Wang, was like. It would be interesting, she felt, to see what would happen if he decided to spit on their living room rug. But Alfred turned out to be a disappointment. He clutched his mother's gown through the whole party and didn't spit once.

While Mrs. Barrett served tea to the mothers, Mr. Barrett helped Christene and Charlotte run the games. One thing that struck Charlotte was how jovial her father seemed to be, even through all the baby games and the messy scene at the birthday table. Chopsticks and chocolate cake turned out to be just as bad as the girls had thought it would be, but it didn't bother Mr. Barrett one bit. He actually seemed thrilled at seeing the cake and frosting smeared all over everything. And the closer the time came for the Pa Hsi Man to appear, the more joyful he became. He really *must* want to see the Pa Hsi Man, Charlotte told herself in surprise.

Charlotte loved the Chinese magic man, too, with his flowing satin suit, nimble feet, and flashing black eyes. But today she chewed her lower lip with nervous impatience as she sat on the floor watching him. When he swallowed bright balls of flaming fire, turned green silk scarves into red ones, purple scarves into orange ones, and made his pet monkey disappear into an old trunk only to reappear on his shoulder a few minutes later calmly eating a peanut, Charlotte gritted her teeth over the amount of time he was taking.

"Lun dun, lun dun! Eega lun dun!" cried the Pa Hsi Man. Hard to do, hard to do! One piece hard to do!

He was starting his final trick at last, the one that would end with Jamey and his guests each receiving a surprise present. Charlotte knew the trick, because she and Christene had had it at their parties when they were younger. Exchanging secret glances with Christene, she rose quietly and edged toward the door leading to the back stairs.

"Lun dun, lun dun! Eega lun dun!" said the Pa Hsi Man again. He took from his trunk a large sheet of multicolored paper, wadded it into a ball, and swallowed it. Then, after making a huge pretense of coughing and sputtering, he began to draw colorful serpentine paper from his mouth, yards and yards of it.

Though Charlotte knew exactly what was going to happen, she stood poised at the door, hypnotized by the paper piling up on the floor. When the end of the serpentine finally drifted down from his mouth, and the Pa Hsi Man looked in mock dismay at the huge mound of paper in front of him, the children clapped and giggled uproariously. Charlotte knew she ought to leave, but for some strange reason, she was unable to pull herself away, and waited for the words, "Lai la! Lai la!" meaning "Come! Come!" which the Pa Hsi Man would call out, inviting the children to come and dig under the paper for their gifts.

But the magic man never said the words. Instead, he made a sign to his monkey, who leaped lightly from his shoulder to the floor and dived into the paper mound. The mound began to quiver and shake as if it were a volcano about to erupt. Then the monkey poked his head through the paper, looked mischievously

around the room, and a moment later walked proudly out, leading at the end of a narrow red leather leash— a puppy!

The puppy was small and black, but he did not have a white nose, nor was he fuzzy like a ball of wool. This puppy's hair was shiny and wavy, and he had long ears that almost reached to the floor. This was somebody's puppy, all right, but he wasn't Charlotte's Maximilian.

Charlotte looked at Christene to see what she knew about it, but Christene only turned toward her with a blank look and a shrug.

Curiously, Charlotte watched to see what the monkey would do next, and saw him hesitate, turn to the magic man, and then, at a sign from his master, lead the puppy to Jamey. Only instead of doing a trick, as Charlotte expected he would, the puppy simply wagged his whole hind end, whimpered joyfully, and made a puddle on the rug.

As Liu rushed out with a rag, Charlotte looked at her mother and father to see what *they* were going to do about it. But all her mother did was smile at Mr. Barrett, while he in turn beamed at the puppy and Jamey. And then, suddenly, Charlotte knew! Before her father actually said the words, she knew.

"Well, Jamey, don't just sit there looking at him. Take him! He's yours, son. Happy birthday!"

Jamey, who had been sitting and looking at the puppy with wide eyes and open mouth, suddenly grabbed him and hugged him.

"Jamey, I want to pet him!"

"No, I want to!"

"I said first!"

The children crowded around Jamey.

"Lai la! Lai la!" the Pa Hsi Man now cried, inviting them to find their gifts under the mound of serpentine, but no one paid any attention to him.

Charlotte stood in the doorway, too stunned to move. Then, when she saw Christene looking in her direction, she beckoned frantically. Christene rose and threaded her way around the excited children to Charlotte.

"Chrissy, what are we going to do?" Charlotte whispered hysterically.

"Nothing, I guess," said Christene.

"But we have to do something, Chrissy. We can't just do nothing!" Charlotte wanted to scream this, but she couldn't, not with all those people there.

"Well, I'm going to do nothing, Charlie," Christene said, her voice strangely cold, as if she didn't even care. But she added more gently, "Come on, we might as well go see the puppy. I think he's a cocker spaniel. He's cute, Charlie. He really is cute."

Of course, the puppy was cute. All puppies were cute. But how could she calmly "go see the puppy," some other strange puppy that was not Maximilian? Not poor little black woolly Maximilian, who was to have been the center of attention, little wonk Maximilian, little mongrel Maximilian, sitting and waiting trustingly in the basement.

As Christene turned away, Charlotte saw their father grinning and waving at them to come over. But Charlotte ignored him and turned and fled blindly up the stairs, tears already streaming down her cheeks before she reached the top.

Liar! Traitor! Coming to Jamey's party just to see the Pa Hsi Man! That was a lie. Her father was a liar. And giving Jamey a puppy without telling the girls when they'd been begging for one for years. Traitor!

Charlotte raced down the hall and fell on her bed. She hated her father! She would never trust him again. And she hated the strange puppy. She could never love him, never! She would never love anyone!

Charlotte lay on her bed waiting for someone to miss her and come for her so that she could make these terrible pronouncements. But no one came. She felt as if she had been there for hours before she finally heard footsteps coming down the hall. And then it was only Christene's voice that said, "Charlie, what's wrong? You've been gone for fifteen minutes. Daddy thought you'd come up to the bathroom, but that's a long time to be in the bathroom."

Christene was the wrong person to have come. She wasn't the one Charlotte wanted to blow up at. After all, it wasn't Christene's fault.

Charlotte grunted into the pillow.

"You ought to come see the puppy, Charlie. He—he really is cute." Christene was trying. She was really trying, and Charlotte felt she could hardly continue to lie there sniffing and saying nothing.

"Did—did you tell them about my puppy?"

"No. They're busy with the company right now. I couldn't, Charlie."

"Do you think they'll let us keep him?"

"No," said Christene honestly. "They'll make Dossafoo take him back. You know they won't let us have two dogs."

Charlotte did know it and began to sniff again.

"It isn't any good to cry, Charlie. It won't make any difference. You'll just have to forget about it."

"I won't forget about it. I won't forget about Maximilian. He—he was *my* dog!" As soon as she'd said this, Charlotte knew it was a mistake.

"I thought he was supposed to be a present for Jamey," Christene snapped back quickly.

"Well, I don't care," said Charlotte, not concerned that this retort didn't make any sense. "They're not going to take him away. They're not going to!"

"You don't have to scream at me!" Christene said. "My ears are perfectly good."

"I'm not screaming!" screamed Charlotte.

"Yes, you are! You're being a baby, Charlie. You sound just like a baby." Christene strode to the door, stood there for a moment, then added coolly, "Anyway, I *told* you it wouldn't work."

This was the final blow.

"Stink!" Charlotte shouted through the doorway at Christene in as loud a voice as she dared. But if Christene heard her, she paid no attention and went right on walking down the hall.

SIX

WHEN the birthday party was over, Charlotte went on sobbing so desperately that for a while she was the center of sympathetic attention. But Christene was right—crying didn't do any good. All Charlotte accomplished was to exact from her parents a promise that they would try to find Maximilian a good home, and that was all. He still had to go back, and that, they said, was final. He had to go back at once, in fact, before anyone (meaning Charlotte) became unnecessarily attached to him. So Dossafoo was instructed to return Maximilian to the compradore that same evening. Charlotte continued to be a pest on the subject, however, even after he was gone, and finally even the sympathy ended.

"If you don't stop talking about it, Charlie, you might as well go to your room," Mrs. Barrett said at the dinner table. "We've heard enough!"

Charlotte pushed her chair noisily away from the table and stomped upstairs, where she moped for an hour. Finally she couldn't stand being by herself any longer and stomped back down again. Dusty, the cocker spaniel puppy, had been brought from his quarters in the guest bathroom off the front hall and was now waddling around on a large carpet of newspapers spread across the living room. Except for Charlotte, the whole family was sitting on the floor around him, Jamey howling with laughter because Dusty insisted on trying to leave the newspapers. Both Liu and Amah Cho Mei stood by anxiously clutching towels in case he did. They were all having a marvelous time, and nobody seemed to notice Charlotte's arrival.

Charlotte had made such a big show of not being interested in "that dog" that she walked self-righteously past everyone with her book, and on into the den. There, in plain sight of her family, she flopped down in a chair and pretended to read.

"Charlie, come see my puppy," Jamey finally called to her.

Charlotte turned a page studiously as if she were completely lost in her story, and didn't reply.

"Why doesn't she answer?" Jamey asked.

"Your sister has other things on her mind," Mrs. Barrett said. "Just don't bother her."

"She'll get over it," Charlotte heard her father say.

Actually, she was already over it. She hated not being a part of the family, even though she'd done the deed herself, and now she was dying to have a closer look at "that dog." After all, she was wild about animals, *all* animals, and she knew she was only hurting herself by sulking. But the longer Charlotte sat, the more difficult it became. Finally, she marched upstairs again. Completely miserable, she drew her bath in the big claw-footed iron tub in their bathroom, undressed, climbed in, sat gloomily for ten minutes without washing herself, climbed back out, and got ready for bed. She considered making herself a cup of hot chocolate, then remembered that on top of everything else, she had to stay out of the kitchen for a month. A bargain was a bargain, and Dossafoo had kept his end of it. She felt she ought to, too.

Charlotte hoped that when Christene arrived to go to bed, she would be kind and somehow help to end this terrible problem. But when Christene did come into the room already in her pajamas, she had something else to speak to Charlotte about.

"Charlie, if there's anything you think you might need in this room between two and four o'clock tomorrow afternoon, I'd like it if you could get it so you wouldn't need to come in then."

"Why?" asked Charlotte.

"Because Moira is coming over," said Christene, "and since it's Sunday and there's no place else for us to be alone, Mother said we could have tea brought up here."

"Why can't you use the playroom?" Charlotte asked, only arbitrarily choosing to name the playroom. She really didn't see why they needed to be alone in any room.

"Oh honestly, Charlie. Moira and I are in the eighth

grade. We're *not* going to sit in the playroom. Now, are you going to promise to stay out of the bedroom tomorrow afternoon or not?"

"I guess so," said Charlotte.

Christene climbed into bed and fluffed up her pillow determinedly. "Well, you'd better!"

Moira! That was something else to think about. So far the problem had been remote, something that happened only in school or in Moira's house. Charlotte could afford to be generous about it then. But now it was beginning to move into their own house, into Charlotte and Christene's own room. And it seemed that Charlotte could do nothing about it.

By the time Moira arrived, Charlotte was convinced that her sister had gone a little batty over the whole idea. She'd gone around instructing everyone, not just Charlotte, on how to behave in front of Moira, as if Moira were royalty. Charlotte personally planned to stay as far away from Moira as possible, even without Christene's instructions.

Still, it wasn't half an hour after Christene and Moira had disappeared into the room that Charlotte remembered she'd left her copy of *Little Women* under the bed. Finally she gathered up enough courage to knock on the bedroom door.

"Who is it?" Christene called out in a sweet voice.

"It's me. I forgot something, Chrissy. May I come in?"

There was a long pause. "What did you forget?" Christene asked suspiciously.

"My *Little Women*. Chrissy, let me come in. Please!"

"Oh, all right, but hurry up!"

Both girls were sitting on the beds—Moira, her feet curled up under her, on Charlotte's very own bed! A deadly silence greeted Charlotte as she came in and fumbled under her bed for her book.

"Please shut the door when you leave," Christene said stiffly. "And shut it tight!"

Biting her lip to keep from making an angry retort, Charlotte banged the door shut, then strode downstairs and dropped in front of the fireplace. She would have loved to stop first to see Dusty, asleep in the bathroom in his basket, but she was still stubbornly refusing to have anything to do with him. She wanted desperately to break down and wished that she had at the beginning when everyone was being nice about it. Now nobody seemed to want to help her, and it had become impossible.

But it was nice in the den, peaceful and quiet. Liu and Coolie had been working there earlier, stuffing cotton batting around the windows to protect the house against the Gobi winds that would soon begin to blow, bringing in cold and dust. Before they had left, they had built a fire in the den fireplace, and the small egg-shaped coals gave off a warm, comfortable glow. Jamey was in his room with Amah, and Mr. and Mrs. Barrett were still upstairs taking Sunday naps. Charlotte, alone in the den, settled down on her stomach before the fireplace, prepared to read pages and pages of *Little Women*. She'd been reading only a few minutes, though, when Jamey came bursting into the room, his arms laden with toys.

"Jamey, you were supposed to stay in your room

while Christene has her guest," Charlotte said. Since her own room was being so unfairly occupied, she didn't see why she couldn't at least have the den to herself for a while.

"Well, I didn't stay in it," said Jamey, and he began to run his red truck around the rug.

Charlotte tried to pretend he wasn't there and went on with her reading. After a few moments, though, she felt something hit her leg. Then more things hit her leg, harder. Reaching down, she closed her fingers around three small round wrinkled balls. They were walnuts. Charlotte examined them and found the faces she had drawn on them for Jamey weeks ago. Now Jamey was pelting her with them.

"Jamey, stop it!"

"I'm not doing anything," said Jamey playfully.

"Yes, you are. You are! You are!" Charlotte shot back furiously.

"No, I'm not," said Jamey.

Charlotte gritted her teeth. "Yes—you—are!" Suddenly all the anger inside her boiled up—anger at Moira, at Christene, at her father, at Jamey, especially at Jamey because he'd been born a boy and been given the puppy Charlotte had always wanted for herself. She picked up the walnuts and hurled them into the fireplace. Old and dry, they began to burn immediately.

At first, Jamey only sat in stunned silence. Then he let out a piercing scream. He screamed and screamed, and finally began to sob. It wasn't just the ordinary crying of a small boy who'd lost a toy. It was a terrible kind of crying, and it frightened Charlotte. She grabbed the poker and tried to fish the walnuts from the fireplace, but it was too late. They were already making three bright little flames among the coals.

"Jamey, they were only walnuts," Charlotte said desperately.

"No, they were faces! You killed my faces. You drawed them, Charlie. You drawed them for me! Why did you kill them?"

Charlotte had carelessly drawn the faces for Jamey one afternoon and then forgotten about them. But now she knew that Jamey had made treasures of them, just as she had made treasures of small, unimportant things given her by people *she* cared about—a tiny powder puff from her mother, a pink shell that Christene had found on the beach last summer, a brass bottle top from Dossafoo.

"I'll draw you some more. Jamey, I can draw you lots more walnut faces. They'll be just the same."

"No! No! You can't draw my faces. Mine are dead!"

"Jamey, wait here," Charlotte said. "And please stop crying. I've got something for you. I really have!"

She flew out of the den and up the stairs, bumping into her mother and father and Amah Cho Mei, all coming down to see what the commotion was about.

"Jamey's all right. Jamey's all right," Charlotte said, more to herself than to any of them. Brushing by them, she raced down the hall and burst into the bedroom without bothering to knock. From the corner of her eye, she saw Christene and Moira quickly turn face down tablets of paper they'd been writing on. Christene's face had turned a bright red. She looked guilty—and furious.

"You didn't knock, Charlie! And you'd just better leave."

"I'm sorry, Chrissy. I have to get something first." Charlotte knelt in front of the chest of drawers, pulled open the bottom drawer, and took out a square blue tin box. It had once held Huntley & Palmer tea biscuits, but now it was Charlotte's treasure box. Quickly she removed the top and took from the box a tiny red clay squirrel that had come from a snapper at one of Christene's birthday parties. Throwing the box back into the drawer, she jumped up and raced out of the room, forgetting entirely about shutting the door. She heard it slam behind her as she ran down the stairs.

In the den, Mrs. Barrett and Amah were consoling Jamey. Mr. Barrett was stooped in front of the fireplace, poking the coals ruefully. All three turned questioning, accusing looks at Charlotte as she ran in. Charlotte started toward Jamey with the squirrel tightly clutched in her hand, but with all of them staring at her, she stopped suddenly, unable to move.

"Charlie, why did you throw something that belonged to Jamey into the fire?" Mrs. Barrett asked, just as Charlotte knew someone would.

"Because," replied Charlotte, her fingers squeezing around the squirrel in a tight fist.

" 'Because' isn't an answer," her mother said. "You'll have to do better than that."

Charlotte clamped her teeth together and shrugged. She knew she could have said, "Jamey started it," and then it would have been her word against Jamey's, but remembering Jamey's terrible scream of despair at losing his "faces," she couldn't do it. So she simply stood with her gaze glued to the fireplace.

"Look at me, Charlie," Mrs. Barrett said sternly.

Charlotte gave her mother one quick glance and then went back to staring at the burning coals.

All at once, her father stood up and said, "Sue, why don't you and Amah take Jamey upstairs. Charlie and I have something to talk over."

"Oh," said Mrs. Barrett, hesitating. "Well, all right. Come along, Jamey." Together with Amah Cho Mei, she herded Jamey, still sniffling miserably, out of the room.

When they'd gone, Mr. Barrett sat down comfortably in his chair and held out his arms to Charlotte. "Come here, sweetheart."

Dragging her feet, Charlotte moved slowly toward her father and felt herself being pulled down onto his lap. She didn't struggle to get away. This was one lap she had always liked to sit on. It was big and comfortable and protecting. And suddenly finding herself there after all that had happened, Charlotte couldn't hold out any longer. She threw her face into her father's old woolly gray sweater and burst into tears.

Her father just sat holding her, saying nothing. Then, when she'd quieted down, he said, "There, you feeling better?"

Charlotte nodded. "I didn't mean to do it, Daddy. It just happened."

"I know," her father said quietly. He squeezed Charlotte's shoulders. "Say, what's that you have all clutched up in your fist?"

Charlotte uncurled her fingers. "A little squirrel. Jamey's always wanted it. I was going to give it to him."

"He'll like that."

"Will it make up for the walnut faces?" Charlotte asked.

"It won't replace them, if that's what you mean," Mr. Barrett said. "When something's happened, it's happened. When something's gone, it's gone. But"—he smiled—"you can still give the squirrel to Jamey for another reason."

"What's that?"

"Well, to let him know you love him a little."

"Oh, I love him a lot!" Charlotte said quickly, quite sure now that she did. "It's just that—"

"Just that what, kitten?"

"Daddy"—Charlotte hesitated—"why do you like boys better than girls?"

"Who ever said I did?"

"Well, if you don't, why did you have it all planned to call Christene, Christopher, and me, Charles, before we were born?"

"Great scott, where did you get an asinine idea like that, Charlie?"

"Chrissy told me."

"Well, Chris shouldn't go around peddling information she knows nothing about." Mr. Barrett shook his head. "I wonder how she dreamed that up?"

Charlotte shrugged. "But, Daddy, if you don't like boys better than girls, why did you—why did you get Jamey that puppy and not us?" Charlotte spilled this out in a hurry.

"So that's it!" said Mr. Barrett. He shifted in his chair so that he was leaning on the opposite arm and looking right at Charlotte. "See here, kitten, did it ever occur to you what a closed corporation you and Chris have always been? Here's poor old Jamey, the odd man out. What's he supposed to do when you and Chris go into one of your famous huddles?"

"*I* play with Jamey, Daddy."

"I know you do sometimes, but there are those other times! I just thought it would be nice for Jamey to have a dog, that's all. And I got him a cocker spaniel because that's what I had when I was a boy."

"Oh," said Charlotte, studying the squirrel in her hand.

"Anyway, don't you think you've been on your high horse about this thing long enough? You know, Dusty is technically Jamey's dog, but as I've explained to Jamey, he's really the family dog. He belongs to all of us. Why don't you come along with me now, and we'll go see him."

Charlotte hesitated for only about half a second before jumping up. With her father holding her hand, she walked to where Dusty lay asleep in his basket. Dropping down on her knees beside him, she began to stroke his long, silky ears.

"He's beautiful, Daddy. But—"

"But what, Charlie?"

Charlotte shrugged her shoulders helplessly. "He isn't Maximilian."

"I know," Mr. Barrett said simply, and Charlotte felt she could hug her father. He really *did* know.

"Daddy, will you promise to find him a good home?"

"I've already promised. And I've given Dossafoo money to see that the compradore takes care of him until we do find a home. I'll check down there personally. But in the meantime, you don't suppose you could learn to love this puppy—just a little?"

"Oh, I think so," Charlotte said. She leaned over, rubbed her face against the puppy's silky black head, then grinned up at her father. "Just a little!"

Charlotte was so happy she could hardly sit still long enough at the dinner table to eat. She was finally "off her high horse"; Jamey was thrilled with his squirrel, wouldn't let it out of his sight, and even now had it in front of his place at the table; and a long evening of playing with the new puppy stretched ahead of her. Christene hardly spoke to her, but Charlotte didn't much blame her. She *had* been a pest and was sorry about it, but she intended to apologize for that later. Then they would play with the puppy together and the whole thing would be forgotten. Oh, that puppy! thought Charlotte. She excused herself from the table and raced off to see him.

"Come on when you're through, Chrissy," she called over her shoulder.

But Christene never did come. Jamey came, though, and after he'd left, so did a surprise visitor, Dossafoo.

"Missy Charlie can do, can come kitchen," he said.

"Not for a month," Charlotte told him. "I promised. It's not your fault we couldn't keep the other puppy."

"Not your fault, too," said Dossafoo. "Never mind promise. Can come kitchen now. Kitchen not all same without Missy Charlie make mess!"

Bursting to tell Christene about the new developments, Charlotte decided she couldn't wait for her sister and galloped upstairs to find her. But at the top of the stairs, something brought her to a sudden stop. From behind her parents' closed bedroom door, she had heard Christene's voice.

"Mother, she won't mind!"

She won't mind? Who won't mind? thought Charlotte. She moved closer to the door.

"Of course she'll mind!" This voice belonged to Mrs. Barrett. "Chris, you girls have shared a bedroom since Charlie was born. You can't expect her to like this."

"Well—well, I don't care if she does or not. Oh, Mother, she was such a pest this afternoon, bursting in and out of our room when Moira and I wanted to be alone. And the first time was to get her copy of *Little Women*. Mother, she's already read it four times!"

"Yes, I know, dear," said Mrs. Barrett. "Still, I'm sure if you talked it over with her—explain how you feel—"

"I don't want to talk and explain anything. It's no use. Moira and I are in the eighth grade. Charlie is just a—just a baby. Mother, she doesn't even have a bust!"

This agonized outburst was followed by a moment of stunned silence.

"A what?"

"A bust! Mother, don't you know what a bust is?"

"Of course, I know what it is!" This with some degree of indignation. "But, dear, is that what—what you and Moira spend your time—discussing?"

There was a long pause, and Charlotte moved closer to the door. "Well, not exactly. But that's not the point. It's that—it's that I'm growing up and Charlie hasn't even started yet. She's absolutely flat, Mother!"

Charlotte, poised outside the closed door, looked

down at herself. It was true. She was absolutely flat. But what was wrong with that? The famous movie star Shirley Temple was absolutely flat, too. Of course, she was only six. Still, was that why Christene crept into the bathroom every day to dress and undress, because she was getting a bust and Charlotte wasn't?

"But, Chris, dear, Charlie does understand things. At least we've had our little talk." Mrs. Barrett sounded faint and limp.

"Oh, Mother!" said Christene.

"And then," Mrs. Barrett marched on weakly, "we will be leaving for Peitaho in June, and you'll be leaving for Peking and high school after that, so it's only a few more months really and—and— Oh, all right, dear, don't look at me like that. I suppose we can manage it. Will you want to stay on in the bedroom or take over the playroom?"

"Well, I'd like to have the bedroom because there's the dresser in it, but"—Christene hesitated—"I guess I could let Charlie choose."

Charlotte had heard enough. Silently she crept away from the closed door.

It wasn't until late that night, as she lay awake listening to the soft breathing of Christene asleep in the bed beside hers, that the tears she had so determinedly held back all evening poured down her cheeks. But she hadn't cried when Christene had made the announcement about the room! She had been terribly cool about it. Christene must have been surprised at how *un*-babyish she'd been, but not surprised enough to change her mind about wanting her own room.

The sound of the funeral horns still wailing on the

last night of Great-great-grandfather Yueh's funeral penetrated the room. Charlotte had never minded the sound before, or any of the strange sounds that filled the night, because she could always look across at Christene sleeping peacefully, and feel comforted. Charlotte looked at her sister, wondering what it would be like to have no bed beside hers, to have no one there. And suddenly the eerie sound of the horns was terrifying.

She rolled over onto her stomach and pulled the pillow over her head to drown it out. I can't do it! I can't be alone without Chrissy forever and ever, she thought. No can do, Missy Charlie. No can do! But Charlotte knew that she would have to do. If it meant sleeping with the pillow over her head for the rest of her life, somehow she would have to do.

SEVEN

WITHIN a week, Charlotte was transplanted into the playroom, and by Christmas she'd almost begun to feel that she'd been alone in a room all her life. She wasn't sure whether she liked it or not, but at least she was growing used to it.

And she had to admit that everything had been done to make the move as painless as possible for her, including a huge fuss over new curtains for the playroom. Charlotte was allowed to choose any color she wanted, and quickly chose blue. Their bedrooms had always been pink because that was Christene's color. Along with everything else that was Christene's first choice because she was the older, Charlotte had never questioned the right to choose the bedroom color. Their playrooms had always been white. Nobody knew why and nobody cared. But the bedroom was another matter. And now Charlotte was going to have blue curtains, and even a new bedspread appliquéd with blue daisies.

"Could I have the walls painted blue, too?" Charlotte asked, not really expecting that a wild request like that would be granted.

"Why, of course, dear," said Mrs. Barrett. Within forty-eight hours, Coolie was painting the playroom, now renamed Charlotte's bedroom, a lovely pale blue.

For a brief time, Charlotte had the marvelous feeling that anything she wanted would miraculously come to pass. But this didn't last long. Once she was settled in her new quarters, her position as a favored child soon ended, and things reverted to normal.

Charlotte discovered two nice things about being in the playroom, besides having everything blue. One was that she liked waking up in the morning and finding herself surrounded by all the familiar toys—the cheerful face of her old teddy bear rising up over the huge red bow she'd tied around his neck the Christmas before; the exciting dollhouse made by a clever Chinese carpenter who had furnished the rooms with tiny, intricate furniture matching their own; the "infirmary" of cigar-box beds where all the Barrett dolls had always gone when they'd contracted unbelievably terrible diseases, mostly invented by Charlotte; and the family of Chinese dolls lined up on the windowsill, mother, father, and three children, their soft cloth bodies clothed in bright satin jackets and black cotton trousers and with shiny white faces painted on their composition heads. (Charlotte had always wondered why the faces were white and not yellow.) There was something very comforting about the old toys, and Charlotte was glad that Christene, now suddenly grown-up and dignified and possessed of a bust, didn't want any of them in her room. Will I want to give up my toys one day? Charlotte wondered. Never! she told herself.

The second good thing about the move to the playroom, Charlotte discovered, was that she could stand at the open window at night and, by leaning out and looking past Jamey's room and her parents' room, see the upstairs windows of the Yueh mansion all lit up, with shadowy figures passing behind them. Charlotte could probably have done this before, but somehow she had never thought of it. Now, alone in the playroom at night, as soon as she'd turned out her light, she would tiptoe softly and secretly to her window and stare at the lighted windows across the street.

"One day soon when mourning for Grandfather end, big wedding procession come from Yueh house. Number-three Yueh daughter get married," Dossafoo said to Charlotte in the kitchen one afternoon. She was helping him shell peanuts, but eating more than she was shelling.

"Dossafoo, what is a Chinese wedding like?" Charlotte asked. Because of the processions, which were all she had ever seen of them, Chinese weddings had always interested her enormously. Now she was finding out that one of the shadows she'd been watching at the Yueh mansion belonged to a girl, not too many years older than herself probably, who would soon sit stiffly behind the closed doors of a bright red sedan chair being carried to her wedding.

Dossafoo shrugged. "Dossafoo never marry. But

Chinese wedding very expensive. Many people pay, pay, pay!"

"But what's it like? What do they do?" Charlotte persisted.

"Very expensive," said Dossafoo, shaking his head. It seemed to be the only information he could offer on the subject.

Charlotte ran upstairs to look for her mother, whom she found sitting at her desk, pencil in hand, puzzling over the compradore order book.

"Mother," Charlotte said excitedly. "Did you know that the Number-three Yueh daughter was getting married?"

"No, dear, I don't believe I did," Mrs. Barrett murmured.

"Well, she is. Dossafoo told me," said Charlotte.

"Hmmm," said Mrs. Barrett. "I'm not surprised, Dossafoo being the number-one neighborhood gossip. I would almost expect he knew about the wedding before the Yuehs did!"

Charlotte plunked her elbows on top of the desk and twisted her neck to see what her mother was putting down in the book. "I wonder who she's marrying?"

"Oh, I'm sure her family has picked someone nice for her. She'll like him when she meets him," said Mrs. Barrett vaguely, scratching out a word in the middle of a page.

"Mother! Do you mean Number-three Yueh daughter doesn't know who she's marrying?" This was almost a shriek, and Mrs. Barrett finally laid down her pencil with a sigh.

"Charlie, it's quite possible. Of course, on the other hand," Mrs. Barrett continued reflectively, "in a wealthy family like the Yuehs, the young girl's husband will more than likely come from a family they've known for years, so he won't be a total stranger to her. Still, dear, in a Chinese family that follows the old customs, the mother and father do arrange the marriage."

"Do you mean that Number-three Yueh daughter has to marry *that man* whether she wants to or not?"

Mrs. Barrett smiled at Charlotte. "Whether or not," she said, and picked up her pencil again.

Charlotte gazed off into space, too stunned for a moment to continue the conversation. "Mother, were Mrs. Chen's and Mrs. Loo's husbands arranged for them?" The Chens and the Loos were lively, attractive friends of the Barrett family whom Charlotte especially liked.

"Oh no, dear!" Mrs. Barrett laughed. "The Chens and the Loos are what you would call modern Chinese. I think both couples met in college. The Yuehs do live in a modern European-style house, but from what I can tell, they still observe the very ancient Chinese customs."

"Is that why we don't know them, because they're not modern?" Charlotte asked.

"I've never stopped to think about it. We just don't know them, that's all."

"Yes, but why don't we?" insisted Charlotte.

"Because we've never met them! There, does that satisfy you?" Mrs. Barrett laid her pencil back down on the desk, this time with a little annoyed tap. "Charlie, this is a very formal country. The Chinese have special set ways of doing things. I can't just run across the street and borrow a cup of sugar from Mrs. Yueh simply to—to see what she looks like."

"Couldn't you borrow a cup of—of bean curd?" asked Charlotte.

"Now you're being silly," replied Mrs. Barrett, and up came the pencil again.

Charlotte didn't think she was being silly at all. Many miles away, many months ago, a girl named Doris had said they were odd because they lived in China. Well, they might not be odd just because of that, but it was odd that they should live right across the street from a family and not even know them.

"Well, it's—it's odd!" said Charlotte.

"Now that's a funny word to choose," said Mrs. Barrett. "Anyway, I don't see what's so odd about it. The Yuehs simply lead a very private life, that's all. If you'd stop to think about it, we don't know any of the families on this street."

It was true. Charlotte couldn't argue it. Still, did that make things any less odd? High gray pebbled walls and high red brick walls separated all the families on the street from each other. It was as if everyone were hiding from everyone else.

"But for goodness sake," Mrs. Barrett said, "why all this sudden interest in the Yuehs?"

"Oh, I don't know," said Charlotte indifferently. She had the feeling that it wouldn't be wise to report that she'd been spying on the Yuehs when she was supposed to be in bed at night. Besides, her mother might ask why, and Charlotte didn't know why. It was a strange fascination and curiosity she felt way deep down that would be impossible to explain.

Now Number-three Yueh daughter was being married, and it was clear that unless some miracle happened, Charlotte would never know any more about her than she had known about Great-great-grandfather Yueh, who had died. All she would know of the wedding was what went on outside the gray walls—the procession forming; the people dressed in shimmering pinks and reds, peacock blues, and emerald greens; the musicians playing the strange Oriental music on instruments that still sounded foreign to her ears, though she'd heard them all her life. Charlotte wondered what she would be doing now if she were Number-three Yueh daughter getting ready to marry a man "arranged" for her by her parents. What ancient customs, some hundreds or thousands of years old, were being carried on now inside the walls? Charlotte's mother and father might be very matter-of-fact about all of it, but Charlotte couldn't be.

"Mother, Dossafoo doesn't know anything about Chinese weddings," Charlotte said suddenly.

"I'm not surprised, a crusty old bachelor like Dossafoo."

"Do you? Do you know any more things, Mother? I mean, about the ancient wedding customs and things like that?"

"No, I'm afraid I don't. No more than what I've told you. But if you're so interested, perhaps you could talk to Mrs. Chen or—or why don't you ask Anna in your class at school? That's a good idea, don't you think?"

Mrs. Barrett's voice drifted away as she stared once again with a puzzled frown at the notebook in front of her.

Charlotte left, without trying to explain to her mother that the idea of discussing weddings with Anna wasn't good at all. In fact, it was impossible.

Charlotte and Anna's conversations with each other were all terribly formal (yes, wasn't that the word her mother had used?), as if they'd just met, and they were always about schoolwork. Charlotte couldn't imagine talking about anything else with Anna. The situation with Anna was like the one with the Yuehs, people hiding behind high walls. They had met, but that was all. They were classroom acquaintances, not friends.

Actually, all Charlotte had was acquaintances. There were some girls in both the fifth and seventh grades whom Charlotte played games with at recess, but they all had their special friends in their own classes. Charlotte was nobody's special friend at school. And now she was nobody's special friend at home, either, unless you counted Jamey, which Charlotte didn't. With her, Christene was the one who counted. These days Christene was friendly enough with Charlotte, but things were simply different from the way they had been, and Charlotte knew they would never be the same again.

And then it was Christmas, and suddenly, things *were* the same again.

For Charlotte, Christmas was always the most exciting, glowing, special time of her life—hurtling downstairs every morning to read the little box on the front page of the newspaper that said how many shopping days were left until December twenty-fifth, stockings hung at the foot of their beds Christmas Eve, the giant spruce tree a blaze of light from hundreds of candles lit by the servants before the children were allowed to see it, the familiar ornaments that came from the same yellowed boxes year after year—the swan from Germany with its spun-glass tail, the snappers from England pasted over with paper Santa Clauses, the glass trumpets from Austria. For Charlotte, anything miraculous could be expected to happen at Christmas, and this year it was Christene wanting a doll!

Charlotte wanted a doll, too, but that was no surprise. She had always had a new doll at Christmas, and for Charlotte, when something had always happened, then it would always go on happening. Whether she had given up playing with them or not, she intended to have a new doll every Christmas of her life even if she had to give it to herself. But for the now grown-up Christene to want a new doll? Charlotte could hardly believe it.

The dolls along with other toys had been ordered out of a catalog from America months ago. These dolls would be quite different from anything they had had before, with composition heads but rubber bodies, so they could actually be given a bath. This was very new and very exciting, a doll you could bathe.

"But you don't have to have it, you know," Mrs. Barrett told Christene. "I can always save it for a birthday gift for someone."

"No, I want it," Christene said very definitely. But then she said to Charlotte, "Charlie, promise something? Promise me you won't tell Moira. I mean about the doll. She doesn't need to know about it."

"Oh yes, I promise, Chrissy," Charlotte breathed happily. She and Christene were going to have a conspiracy against Moira. Later, they would give the dolls a bath. She and Christene would actually be playing with dolls together once again!

And there was even a second Christmas surprise that happened, all because Christene, unbelievably, said she still wanted to hang a stocking at the foot of her bed.

"I think I should because of Jamey," she said. "He'd wonder why Santa Claus would fill a stocking for him and not for me, too. How would we explain it if I didn't have a stocking?"

Christene was right—how would they? Still, Charlotte had the distinct feeling that Christene would have wanted to hang a stocking anyway, Jamey or no Jamey. But there was a problem about the stockings this year.

Christene and Charlotte had always, all their lives, awakened together Christmas morning, seen the mysterious, lumpy shadows rising up from the foot of their beds, forced themselves to lie there in agonizing suspense, and then finally, when they could bear it no longer, bounced to the foot of their beds with one great swoop. This year, because they were in separate rooms, they would be unpacking their Christmas stockings alone. Charlotte tried to get up the courage to ask Christene if she couldn't move back to her old bed just that one night, but she never did. And finally she didn't need to, because Christene invited her! So they unpacked their stockings together after all, and then went to get Jamey so all three of them, along with Dusty, could sit huddled on the top step waiting for the candles on the tree to be lit, just as they always had.

But as soon as the excitement of Christmas morning was over, Christene seemed to forget about Charlotte. She spent the afternoon with Moira Evans, and that night covered Charlotte's old bed with all her new Christmas things so that there could be no question of anyone spending the night there. Confused and disappointed, Charlotte returned to the playroom.

The situation with Moira seemed to be growing worse instead of better, at least to Charlotte. There was now the telephone. The Barretts were one of the first families in Tientsin to have a telephone put in their home, and Charlotte was wildly excited about it, even though she had no one to call. But Christene did. Now, because of the telephone, Christene's days could begin and end with Moira. It began to seem to Charlotte as if the telephone had been installed expressly for them.

Then there were the lessons. Christene now took piano lessons because Moira was having them. Also ballroom dancing, tap dancing, and ice skating lessons. When you grew up, Charlotte decided, you couldn't do anything just for fun anymore. Everything had to be accomplished through lessons. Naturally, except for piano, the girls took all their lessons together.

And finally, there was something that, like the telephone, was exciting when it began, but that in the end left Charlotte more outside Christene's life than ever.

One afternoon, four days after Christmas, she heard the doorbell ring, and after a few minutes when she could no longer contain her curiosity, she came galloping down the stairs to find Cousin Philip, tall and good looking as ever, standing with her mother in the living room.

"Mother!" Charlotte said indignantly. "Why didn't you tell us?"

Mrs. Barrett shrugged helplessly. "Dear, I didn't know!" This was true. Cousin Philip, Mr. Barrett's young cousin, had written months ago that he had booked passage on the U.S.S. *President Hoover*, arriving the end of January in time for him to begin his new job in Mr. Barrett's office. Here he was, unannounced, a month early. Later, Charlotte knew, someone would say, "Well, that's Philip—unpredictable as usual!" Which was what she liked about him. He didn't seem like the kind of person who had to have lessons in everything.

"Well, I guess you're here," Charlotte said.

"Where else?" said Cousin Philip, holding out his arms toward her.

Charlotte started toward him and then came to a sudden stop. In the past, whenever they'd been on leave in America and Charlotte was seeing her cousin for the first time (at the ages of nine, six, and three respectively), he had always picked her up and swung her, giggling, into the air. But a tall, skinny eleven, she couldn't let that happen now. Embarrassed, wishing she hadn't come tumbling down the stairs like a baby giraffe, she stared down at the hem of her dress. Staring back at her were nearly two inches of hemline that showed clearly where the dress had been lengthened. Charlotte had never minded dropped hemlines showing before, but she did now. Uncomfortably, she looked up at Cousin Philip and was relieved to see that he had lowered his arms to his sides.

"I see what you mean," he said, grinning wryly. Then he walked toward Charlotte with his right hand outstretched, and they shook hands.

But it wasn't until she was curled up on the couch beside her mother, decorously drinking a cup of hot chocolate as Cousin Philip explained how he'd suddenly decided to come earlier so he could learn something of China before going to work, making them laugh at his funny descriptions of the people with whom he'd shared a dining table aboard ship, that Charlotte could forget how uncomfortable she'd felt over the incident.

They hadn't been talking long when Christene returned from her ballet lesson, bringing Moira Evans with her. Charlotte nearly spilled hot chocolate all over the couch, watching Christene introduce Moira to Cousin Philip. Christene stammered as she got mixed up in trying to decide whether to introduce her friend as "Moira" or "Miss Evans." She finally settled on "Miss Evans," so Cousin Philip became "Mr. Barrett." While this was taking place, Moira stood staring at Cousin Philip with big round eyes, occasionally waving her eyelashes at him as if to show that she was only partially paralyzed, and when the introductions were over, she went right on staring at him until even *he* looked uncomfortable.

Charlotte hoped that the two girls would leave as quickly as possible. They usually did as soon as they walked into a room and discovered a member of the Barrett family already in it, particularly Charlotte. But today, when Mrs. Barrett asked, "Wouldn't you girls like to join us here in the den?" to Charlotte's horror, they did, plopping down on the couch beside her as if they were all the closest friends in the world.

In the end, the introduction of Cousin Philip to Moira ruined more than just the afternoon for Charlotte, because it seemed that now Moira was going to spend half her life at the Barrett house.

Charlotte grew thoroughly sick of the new telephone, and of being told, "Charlie, please leave. This is a *private* conversation." Christene hardly needed to be so private, because Charlotte knew exactly what the conversations were about, particularly when the urgent telephone calls made each time Cousin Philip visited their home were followed by the sudden appearance of Moira Evans, wearing sheer silk stockings! Charlotte thought she would collapse at this.

But what disgusted Charlotte most of all was the part her own sister played in Moira's "case" on Cousin Philip. Christene was so wound up in helping the mooning Moira that it was actually affecting her own behavior. Half the time she didn't seem to hear what you were saying to her. If she did hear, it was only to become irritated with whatever you were saying. And Charlotte began to hear dozens of tearful arguments with their mother behind closed doors. After at least one of these arguments, Christene began to appear in silk stockings, too, on the afternoons when Moira came prissing in wearing hers. It was, Charlotte decided, like some kind of rash. Would she, she wondered, break out in sheer silk stockings? She couldn't imagine it. She didn't *want* to imagine it.

Charlotte never gave up hoping that Christene would say once again, "Come spend the night with me in our room, Charlie!" But Christene never did. The excitement of Christmas had ended. The flurry over Cousin Philip's arrival died down. And Charlotte began once again to think about Chinese weddings, about Number-three Yueh daughter, who might soon be marrying a complete stranger. Once again, she began climbing out of bed every night to stare at the lighted windows across the street.

As for Christene's doll, it ended up on a shelf in the playroom. Charlotte took it down once and gave it a bath along with her own doll because she felt sorry for it, but she never told Christene or got her permission. Charlotte didn't think it mattered. Along with everything else, Christene seemed to have forgotten all about it.

EIGHT

CHARLOTTE was awakened by Jamey shaking her shoulder and shouting, "Charlie, it's snow outside! Come see, it's snow!"

Charlotte stretched sleepily and then, finally realizing what Jamey had been saying, threw herself out of bed and ran with him to the window. Snow had fallen during the night, the ground was thick with it, and more was coming down.

Snow wasn't such a surprise in Tientsin, but so much of it was. Every winter they had more than enough wind and Gobi dust biting into their faces and legs like thousands of sharp razor blades, and weather so cold they could ice skate on frozen ponds, but there was never enough snow. They had all hoped it would snow during Christmas vacation, but it hadn't. Now, this was making up for it.

"Charlie, can we go out now?" Jamey danced up and down in front of the window.

"No. We have to go to school. There isn't time. We can play in it at school, though."

"But I want to build a snowman here!" Jamey wailed.

"We'll build one when I get home this afternoon," said Charlotte.

"All right." Jamey nodded agreeably. He studied the snow gathering in a heap on the windowsill, and then announced in a matter-of-fact voice, "Charlie, I'm going to take off my shoes and socks in the snow."

"You can do that this afternoon," said Charlotte calmly. She had tried the same thing herself three years earlier, but decided that it was probably best to let Jamey find out for himself that it was something you only wanted to try once in your life.

"No can do!" Amah Cho Mei's voice burst in on them from behind. "No can take off shoes and socks. You no talk nonsense, Jamey. I tell you mommy. Lai la! Lai la! You come get ready for school."

She herded Jamey out of the room, but as they were going, Jamey turned and grinned wickedly at Charlotte. Jamey was still close to being a baby, but already he had learned how to deal with Amah. Charlotte wondered if she should encourage him in this, but then he was only doing what she and Christene had done. She grinned back at him.

On most mornings now, Christene still walked as far as Moira's house with Charlotte and Jamey, but she was always so slow in getting ready that today Jamey didn't want to wait for her. Neither did Charlotte. She was as anxious as Jamey to be outside, afraid the snow might stop falling before they left the house. But it was still coming down in a soft, thick cloud. Jamey's knitted cap was soon white with it, and his eyelashes were heavy with flakes. Giggling at the way they each looked, they started for school.

Around the bend of the brick wall surrounding their house, they had to make a wide turn to keep from bumping into the hot noodle man, who had wheeled his cart to the street corner and was already doing a brisk business. Without consciously thinking about it, they slowed down going past him, watching him take a dip-perful of sauce from a pot bubbling over the glowing coals of his portable stove and pour it over a bowl of steaming white noodles. His customer, a rickshaw coolie who had parked his rickshaw at the side of the street while he ate his meal, carefully counted out some brown coppers for the noodle man, then took the white china bowl from him along with a pair of chopsticks. The coolie was dressed only in thin faded blue cotton trou-sers and jacket, and even in the snow, wore straw san-dals on his feet with filthy rags wrapped around for socks. Rickshaw coolies led pitifully hard and hungry lives, and Charlotte was glad that this one at least could buy a hearty hot meal from the noodle vendor. He was enjoying it thoroughly, sucking up the noodles noisily, smacking his lips, and grinning over his bowl at the other customers.

Seven or eight Chinese men besides the coolie were clustered around the noodle man's brightly burning stove. They were all dressed in warm padded gray or blue cotton robes, and some wore hats with flaps that came down over their ears. They were laughing and joking with each other, and all shoving noodles into their mouths with as much noise and relish as the rickshaw coolie.

Charlotte couldn't help staring. It didn't seem fair that anything that looked, sounded, and smelled so delicious as a meal from the noodle man should be so forbidden.

"Could we have some?" Jamey asked.

"No!" replied Charlotte fiercely.

"Why can't we ever?"

"You know why," replied Charlotte.

"Cho-le-ra," Jamey said, nodding his head to emphasize each syllable.

Cholera might not be exactly what a person would get, but Jamey was too young to have it all explained to him, and cholera was a good, useful, frightening word.

"Yes," said Charlotte, and let it go at that.

She loved the street vendors, the shopkeepers who carried their miniature shops with them, ready to do business anyplace, anytime. It was impossible to imagine the streets without them—the paper lantern sellers, the menders of boot soles, the sweet sellers with their endlessly fascinating assortment of dried fruits, peanuts, sesame candy, melon seeds, fruit syrups, jujubes, and even drinks like sarsaparilla. And what would Liu, Dossafoo, and Coolie have done without the traveling barber? Or Amah without the dry goods man, who would remove every tray from a neat stack so she could choose one tiny skein of red embroidery thread or a single needle? Yes, it was definitely better to have street vendors and not be allowed to buy from some of them, Charlotte long ago concluded, than not to have them at all.

Suddenly unaccountably happy just because they had seen the noodle man, she turned her face up toward the sky and opened her mouth. "Look, Jamey, look what I'm doing!"

Jamey followed suit, and for a few moments they stumbled along blindly, faces turned to the sky, eyes closed and mouths open, letting the snowflakes fall in. The flakes felt cold and clean, melting on their tongues. Here was something they could eat at last that hadn't been baked or boiled or roasted by Dossafoo in the kitchen, frozen raindrops from the sky.

School looked like a different world when they arrived there. Charlotte couldn't bring herself to rush right into the building, but stood outside the door watching the snow fall thickly on the playground, making a white skeleton of the monkey bars, a smooth white hill of the curved red tiles that capped the playground walls, and walking snowmen of the boys and girls coming through the school gate. Some boys were already throwing snowballs in front of the school door, but it was hard to tell who they were, bundled up in heavy jackets and knitted caps covered in raggedy patches of white.

Another girl stood on the school steps, but with the snow coming down so heavily, Charlotte didn't recognize her at first. Then, surprised, she realized that it was Anna Chung.

Anna had never been to school this early as long as Charlotte had been there, and she never just stood around outside doing nothing. Anna was always studying, even during the minute or two in the morning before the final bell rang, or during recess when she would take her books outside with her.

"Oh, Anna, isn't the snow pretty!" Charlotte said. She wanted to say *something* to Anna, and it was all she could think of.

"Yes, it is lovely," Anna said stiffly, turning her face for only a moment toward Charlotte, then staring ahead once more.

Although Anna was always formal in her manner when she spoke to someone, she was never so stiff and strained as she seemed this morning. Charlotte wondered about it briefly, then decided she wouldn't let it bother her and would see if she couldn't start up a conversation with Anna about something besides schoolwork.

"Where's William today?" she asked brightly. "He isn't sick, is he?"

"No," Anna replied, turning once again to Charlotte. It was only a brief glance, but it was all the time necessary for Charlotte to see that Anna's stiffness was caused by trying to hold back tears. "He is out there!" Anna pointed to where a group of boys was throwing snowballs.

Charlotte counted five boys in the group, all with their backs toward the school building, hurling snowballs at one boy on the other side of them, away from the building. The boy wasn't hurling snowballs back at them, but was clutching his schoolbooks, his head bent down toward them to protect himself and the books from the flying snowballs. Charlotte could see that he was trying to run for the safety of the school, but each time he was driven back by the other boys. The lone boy being pelted with snowballs was William Chung.

"Anna!" cried Charlotte. "You should go call the principal or Miss Bell."

Anna shook her head. "Oh, I could not do that!"

"Well then, I will," Charlotte announced.

"Please do not!" Anna's voice was pleading. She looked terrified. "He will be all right in a minute."

From the looks of things, Charlotte doubted it, but before she had time to argue with Anna, one of the five boys shouted out, "Wamba dzoa! Wamba dzoa! William is a wamba dzoa! Come on, everybody, let's see if William can run faster than a turtle!" The voice belonged to Eddy Schmidt.

In America, if you called someone a run-like-a-turtle, it would just be a teasing joke. But in China, to be compared to a turtle was a terrible insult. Surely, thought Charlotte, William would fight Eddy over this. Instead, when the five boys set out after him, William turned and ran blindly across the playground. In his path lay a large iron ring anchored in cement, put there years ago for what purpose no one could guess, but now covered with snow. William's foot caught in the ring, and he fell headlong onto the ground, his papers flying in all directions.

"Anna, come on! We have to go help him!" Charlotte cried. She beckoned to Anna and started out toward where William lay sprawled on the ground. Anna, slowed down by her long, narrow Chinese gown, followed behind.

Ahead of the girls, the five boys, seeing that the chase had ended, came to a straggling stop. Charlotte was relieved to see that none of the boys was Barry Dameron or Skinny Buttrick. The boys looked at one another as if of unsure what to do next; then they shrugged, and four of them trailed off, halfheartedly throwing snowballs at one another. The boy who stayed behind, looking embarrassed and uncomfortable as Charlotte and Anna arrived, was Eddy Schmidt.

"We didn't mean anything, William," Eddy mumbled. "I'm sorry." He did look sorry. It was hard to be mad at Eddy for very long. He was a good-natured boy, and not really mean. Charlotte had once seen him furious with some boys for tormenting a wonk dog. But Eddy liked to be the big cheese and wasn't very smart, so he did stupid things like this and then was sorry for it.

"Oh, Eddy," Charlotte said disgustedly. "Just look at William's notebook!"

"Aw, it's all right," Eddy said. The notebook probably did look all right to Eddy. His own looked as if rats had nested in it. He reached down clumsily and handed William a sheet torn from the notebook, the neat, precise handwriting on it now all smudged.

"Thank you, Eddy," said William politely. He seemed to be struggling not to cry.

"No, it isn't all right," said Charlotte, seeing William and Anna look with dismay at the remains of the notebook. "William will have to ask his parents to get him a new one."

"Oh no," Anna blurted out. Her face grew pale, and she exchanged a quick, anxious glance with her brother. "It is all right, as Eddy said, Charlie. William does not need to ask for a new notebook. Please, it is all right!"

Charlotte felt that anyone, even Eddy, could see that it wasn't all right, but she didn't know what else to say about it. They continued silently helping William until a catcall rang across the playground.

"Hey, Eddy, come on," Walter Francis hollered.

Eddy handed William a pencil he had found sunk into the snow, and stood up. "I'm sorry, William," he mumbled again and lumbered off.

By then they had gathered up all of William's books and papers, and the three of them started back to the school building. William was still fumbling desperately with the pages of his notebook, trying to straighten them out, but it looked hopeless.

"William, you can tell Miss Bell what happened so she'll know that it wasn't your fault," Charlotte said. She felt very sorry for William.

"I cannot do that," William said, shaking his head rapidly.

"Oh, you don't have to say who did it," Charlotte offered helpfully. She could understand someone not wanting to tell on someone else. "Miss Bell wouldn't make you do that."

"To tell who did it is not the problem," Anna said in a troubled voice. "It is that Miss Bell might sometime tell"—she threw an anguished look at William as if looking for help—"our father!"

"Oh, Anna," Charlotte said laughingly, "your father couldn't mind that much about a notebook. And even if he did, he'd understand when he found out it wasn't William's fault."

"It was William's fault!" Anna's face flushed a deep pink. "And it was mine also!"

"But it wasn't! I saw—" Charlotte began.

"Yes, it was our fault," Anna said slowly and thoughtfully as if she were explaining it to herself. "We came to school early this morning. It is against our father's wishes that we come to school early. We must come to school to study and not to play is what he has ordered. But this morning we hurried through our Chinese lesson and came early. I am older than William and have seen such a thick snow as this, but William has never seen it. He wanted to have some time to be in it before school started, so we disobeyed our father and came early. Yes, it was our fault," Anna repeated. "But perhaps it was more my fault."

"No, no, Anna!" William cried.

"Yes, more my fault because I am the older," said Anna.

This was all impossible for Charlotte to believe—a father who wouldn't allow his children to come to school early because it might give them a few minutes to play, and then so much terror and misery over one silly notebook. What kind of ogre was this Mr. Chung anyway that his children should be so afraid of him?

When they were hanging up their coats in the girls' cloakroom, Charlotte couldn't help blurting out the question. "Anna, don't you mind—don't you mind having to study all the time and—and never being allowed to play?"

"It does not matter whether I mind or do not mind," Anna replied simply. "My father"—she hesitated—"my father is not wrong to ask us to do as he wishes. It is we who are wrong to disobey."

This reply was so startlingly different from the one she or Christene or any of the girls she had ever known would have given that Charlotte could think of nothing more to say about it. But, before they left the cloakroom, a chilling thought struck her.

"Anna, even if William doesn't ask for a new notebook, what if your father sees the old one?"

"Father does not speak English," Anna said, "so he does not often look at our American schoolwork."

"But what if he decides to?" Charlotte insisted.

"Then," Anna said softly, "I think I do not know what would happen." Her black eyes seemed to grow even darker in confusion and misery.

Charlotte wished she hadn't mentioned a problem for which there seemed to be no solution. "Oh well," she said uncomfortably, "you could always just say that William fell." That William fell, Charlotte repeated to herself. In their fear, no one had thought of the simple explanation that William fell!

Anna looked at her with a puzzled frown. "Would that not be a lie?"

"Anna, William *did* fall down, didn't he? You can fall down anytime. I fell down coming to school last year. You remember when my leg was all bandaged up?"

"Yes, I remember."

"Well, that was an accident. William had an accident this morning. He didn't do it on purpose. He just fell down. That isn't a lie."

"Yes, William fell down," Anna said slowly. "William fell down," she repeated as Charlotte had done, only out loud, as if to print it on her mind. "No, it would not be a lie to say that William fell down." At last, shyly, she smiled at Charlotte.

And with the smile, for the very first time, Anna didn't seem like such a stranger anymore, the formal classroom acquaintance she had been all along. Charlotte returned the smile, and together they hurried to their classroom.

Each time that morning when their eyes met, Charlotte and Anna smiled at one another, and for the first time in her life, Charlotte knew what it felt like to share a secret with someone in her own class, a secret that had happened to them together. She didn't want the feeling to end. She wanted it to go on and on. But how to go from almost friends to real friends? In Anna's case, it seemed almost impossible.

If it were only that Anna was frightened of her father, then Charlotte could perhaps side with her against him. But Anna thought her father was right to have all the rules and regulations, and it didn't matter to her that they were unfair. So what Charlotte, or anyone else, thought or said could make no difference.

It was a school rule that all students must leave the classroom at recess. They were expected to go outside unless it was pouring rain, in which case they could go to the library or to the small assembly room downstairs. Anna and William usually went to the library or assembly room, taking their books to study. When the weather was very nice, they might go outside, but always with books. Anna and William Chung huddled spiderlike together on a bench outside the building, scratching away in notebooks or bent over reading, were a familiar sight to everyone.

Today, Charlotte couldn't help hoping that Anna would invite her to join them. She was willing to give up going out in the snow, even spend the whole recess studying, if Anna asked her. But when the recess bell rang, Anna gathered up her books, gave Charlotte a quick, anxious, polite smile, and scurried out of the room without saying anything. It was easy to see that her father and his order to spend all spare time at schoolwork came first, Charlotte second.

Charlotte waited at her desk until the last possible moment, then realized that, except for Miss Bell, she was the only one left in the room.

"Is something wrong, Charlie?" Miss Bell asked. "Hadn't you better run along outside?"

Embarrassed, Charlotte began quickly to gather the papers and pencils from her desk to put them away. Supporting the desk top with her head, busy straightening her papers in the desk, she didn't hear anyone come into the room.

Then, "Yes, Eddy, what is it?" she heard Miss Bell say.

Twisting her head, Charlotte saw Eddy Schmidt in his heavy snow jacket, shifting uncomfortably from one foot to the other in front of Miss Bell's desk.

"Here," he said gruffly, laying something on the desk. "This is for William—to get him a new notebook."

"Why, Eddy, that's very nice," Miss Bell said. "But why do you feel it necessary to get William a notebook?"

"Well—" Eddy shifted to his left foot. "You'll see when you check our notebooks this afternoon, Miss Bell. William's is wrecked. He came to school early this morning and—and—"

"Yes?" Miss Bell questioned.

"We threw some snowballs at him," Eddy broke out gruffly. "Then we chased him, and he fell and wrecked his notebook. It was my idea to chase him. Anyway, this is for a notebook from the supply cupboard. Will you give it to him?"

"Yes, I'd be happy to do that, Eddy." Miss Bell smiled. "But you know you could have just bought the notebook and given it to him yourself without saying anything to me. Didn't you think of that?"

Back went Eddy to his right foot. "I guess so. But I didn't think William would take it from me. Anyway, I wanted you to know he didn't wreck his own book. Will you give it to him?"

"I certainly will, and thank you for telling me about it, Eddy."

Eddy shifted from one foot to the other as if he thought he ought to say something else, then suddenly jammed his cap on his head and thundered out of the room as fast as he could go.

With a wry half smile on her face, Miss Bell rose from her desk.

"Charlie! What are you doing still in the room? You know you're supposed to be out by now. Are you sick?"

Charlotte let her desk top drop with a thud, leaped up, and ran to Miss Bell's desk. "Oh, Miss Bell, I didn't mean to listen to what Eddy was saying, but I couldn't help it. Miss Bell, you weren't supposed to know about the snowballs and William and Anna getting to school early and"—she stopped, seeing the Chinese dollar bill on Miss Bell's desk, crumpled up and raggedy just the way Eddy Schmidt would hand it to someone. "Oh, that Eddy!" Charlotte tightened her lips furiously.

"Eddy does the best he can," Miss Bell said kindly. "But suppose you pull up a chair to my desk, Charlie, and we'll talk this all over, slowly and from the beginning." She sat back down at her desk, waiting patiently for Charlotte to settle herself in a chair. "Now then!"

"Miss Bell," Charlotte said, "it's just—it's just that Anna and William didn't want you to know about William being chased by the boys because then you might find out they came to school early."

"And what if I did find out?" Miss Bell asked.

"Then you might tell their father," cried Charlotte. "Oh, Miss Bell, if he found out, he might do something terrible to them!"

"Is that what they think?"

"Yes. They're scared of him, Miss Bell. They're *scared* of him!"

"Poor children!" Miss Bell's eyes were troubled. "What a dreadful morning this has been for them. The truth is that I'd have no reason to tell their father anything. Poor William! He's such a neat, careful student. I suppose he's miserable wondering what I'll say the next time I check your notebooks. Well"—Miss Bell sighed—"when I give him the new notebook from Eddy, I'll assure him that this will be the end of the incident."

"Perhaps—perhaps you could give him time in class to copy his old work into his new book," Charlotte said eagerly.

"Yes," Miss Bell said, nodding her head thoughtfully, "yes, Charlie, that's a very good idea. Now then, I think that should take care of everything, don't you?"

"Oh yes," said Charlotte. She started to get up, then sat back down again.

Miss Bell laughed. "You mean we haven't taken care of everything?"

"Oh yes," Charlotte said again. "It's just that—Miss Bell, do you know if the Chungs are a modern Chinese family or—or the old-fashioned kind?"

"Why do you ask a question like that, Charlie?"

"Well"—Charlotte hesitated—"there's a Chinese family across the street from us. Their name is Yueh. Anyway, Number-three Yueh daughter is going to be married. My mother says the Yuehs follow ancient Chinese customs, so Mr. and Mrs. Yueh choose the man for Number-three Yueh daughter to marry, and she has to—she has to marry him whether she wants to or not! Miss Bell, will Anna have to marry someone whether she wants to or not?"

"I'm afraid it's more than likely," Miss Bell replied with a rueful smile. "Of course, I haven't met Anna and William's parents, but from what I'm told, I'd say that they were what you just called 'the old-fashioned kind,' especially where Anna is concerned. I understand it was quite a concession for Mr. Chung to allow Anna to come to a foreign school, which she wanted to do very much. Then he made her wait two years so she and William could come together and be in the same class."

"Two years!" Charlotte exclaimed. "Then Anna is— Miss Bell, is Anna thirteen?"

"Yes, I believe she is."

Thirteen! Christene's age! Charlotte couldn't believe it. Anna was barely as tall as Charlotte and, like Charlotte, seemed to be a very young girl, slender as a bamboo reed in her straight Chinese gowns. Yet Charlotte knew that thirteen for a Chinese girl meant being almost grown up, a woman and not a child anymore. Anna was perhaps not much different in age from Number-three Yueh daughter!

"Oh, Miss Bell," Charlotte said, "will she have to leave school to be married?"

"I certainly hope not," said Miss Bell firmly. Then she laughed again. "But, Charlie, you mustn't worry about it because there really isn't anything you can do about it. Anyway, you can be very pleased with what you did to help Anna and William this morning."

Charlotte grinned at Miss Bell, happy with the compliment. "But I wish I could just talk to Anna about—about ancient Chinese wedding customs and—and things like that," she said wistfully.

"Well, why don't you?" Miss Bell asked.

"Because she has to study all the time. Mr. Chung never allows her to play or talk or do anything!"

"Yes, that's right, of course," Miss Bell said vaguely. For a few moments, she sat tapping her desk with a pencil, studying the cover of a geography book on her desk and seeming to have forgotten all about Charlotte. Then she said suddenly, "Charlie, run to the library and get Anna, will you please? Tell her I'd like to see her at once."

Disappointed because it was clear that her questions about Anna had really taken her nowhere at all, Charlotte scraped her chair back and hurried down the hall to the library for Anna.

"Charlie, don't go," Miss Bell said, as Charlotte turned to leave the classroom. "Bring up another chair, won't you please?"

Charlotte dragged up a chair beside Anna and plunked herself down in it. As Miss Bell explained to Anna what she had learned during recess about William's notebook, and how Anna and William had nothing more to fear from the incident, Charlotte kept wondering what she, Charlotte Barrett, was doing there.

"And you'll promise me not to worry any more about it, won't you, Anna?" Miss Bell said finally.

Anna nodded, her pale frightened face turning a warm pink.

"Good!" Miss Bell smiled suddenly. "Now, you're probably wondering why I asked Charlotte to stay, aren't you? Well, it's this. I want to talk to you both *together* about—a very special assignment."

Anna turned her black almond eyes toward Charlotte curiously, but Charlotte could only shake her head and return a blank look. "An assignment?" Charlotte asked.

"Yes," said Miss Bell, still smiling. "Anna, Charlie has told me that she is very much interested in learning about some of the ancient Chinese customs, the wedding customs, for example. I think it's too bad that a young American girl should grow up in this wonderful country wanting to know things like this, but not having someone close to her own age that she could talk to about it, don't you?"

Anna waited a moment, as if she needed to think the question through, and then she nodded.

"I'm sure," Miss Bell continued, "there are many things *you* could tell Charlotte, and perhaps there are things she could tell you, too."

"Oh yes, Miss Bell," Anna said, adding sadly, "if only there were time away from my studies to talk."

"I'm sure you girls could find some time, couldn't you? Perhaps at recess?" said Miss Bell.

"Oh!" The look of terror returned to Anna's eyes. "My father would not allow that. He has said that I must study then, not play or—or talk!"

"Anna, dear," Miss Bell said gently, "your father sent you to this school to study and to learn. But all studying isn't done *in* books, and all learning isn't done *from* books. We study and we learn from others as well, just as you learn, for example, from me."

"But you are my teacher!" Anna exclaimed.

"Yes, but others can be teachers in a sense, too. Anna, your father has entrusted at least part of your education to this school. This means that he expects the school, and me as your teacher, to know what is best for you. Therefore, I am going to make an assignment, a *school* assignment, for both you and Charlie. That is, until further notice you will spend your recess time together, being each other's teacher, learning from one another whatever—well, whatever you want to learn!"

"Oh!" Charlotte threw her hands up to her mouth in an attempt to stifle a happy squeal.

But Anna only sat stiffly in her chair, hands folded in her lap, staring at Miss Bell's green blotter. Then, just before the bell rang, she said, slowly and carefully, "Will we have a test in this, Miss Bell?"

Miss Bell exchanged a twinkling smile with Charlotte. "Oh, I might check up on you from time to time to see how you're coming along," she said, laughing, "but no, no tests, Anna! Now, run along to your desks, both of you!"

The other boys and girls were already coming into the classroom, their faces red from playing in the snow. The two girls pushed their chairs back against the wall and returned to their desks, smiling shyly at one another the whole way.

All the rest of the day Charlotte felt as if she were going to float out of her desk. Now she and Anna were sharing something that wouldn't end with the morning, but would go on, morning after morning. It would be waiting for her when she came to school the very next day.

"See you tomorrow," Charlotte would call out when she left school that afternoon, and Anna would nod at her and smile.

Tomorrow! After only one short day, the word had a whole new meaning for Charlotte. Tomorrow! What a wonderful thing tomorrow could be!

NINE

TOMORROW! It wasn't until Charlotte was two blocks away from school that she remembered it was Friday, and "tomorrow" meant Monday. It didn't matter. It just allowed more time to think about the wonderful thing that was going to happen every day at school. Private "lessons" with Anna! Anna would be her teacher, and she would be Anna's teacher. How, Charlotte asked herself, had Miss Bell thought of such a wonderful idea? And how had it all come about in the first place?

Well, it was Eddy Schmidt really, thought Charlotte with surprise. Dumb old Eddy Schmidt had yelled a Chinese insult at William, then chased him, and then made up for it by getting him a new notebook. Yes, Eddy had started the whole thing! On the way home, Charlotte made two resolutions. One was that she would work extra hard in school to show Miss Bell that she was worthy of the honor of the special assignment, and the second was that she would try to be nicer to

Eddy and listen to all the insults he brought into class, even if they made her ears burn. Poor Eddy! He probably couldn't help it if explaining insults was the only way he knew to be a big cheese. Miss Bell must be right. Eddy did the best he could.

"See you tomorrow! See you tomorrow!" Charlotte sang to herself. She hurried along, anxious now because she remembered that Jamey was waiting to build a snowman with her. Still, she had to stop just one more time along the way, because just on the other side of the bridge crossing the creek, now covered with snow to make it a scene from a fairy tale, was the chestnut man.

The coals in his brazier burned a cheerful red, the chestnuts popping and crackling in the drifts of floating sparks. It was impossible to go marching right by. Charlotte stopped and stared as the chestnut man filled a folded newspaper cone with hot roasted chestnuts. His creased red face, with the flaps of a fur-lined cap drawn down around it, glowed in the light of the burning coals.

When the paper cone was filled, the chestnut man drew a corner of the paper neatly down over it to cover the chestnuts. Then he started to hand it to his customer, a tiny Chinese girl who had stood patiently by her father's side watching the procedure with solemn black shoe-button eyes. But when the chestnut man noticed Charlotte, he grinned at her, proudly displaying two gaping holes where teeth had once been, and instead held the cone out to Charlotte, pointing to it as if to say, "Buy! Buy! Very good!"

Charlotte smiled shyly and shook her head.

"Ai ya!" said the chestnut man, still grinning. Then he gave the cone to the tiny girl, who grabbed it and promptly hid her face in her father's quilted gown so that all that could be seen of her head was two little pigtails wound with red wool sticking straight out into the air.

Hot chestnuts from a newspaper cone, steaming noodles smothered in a fragrant chicken-vegetable sauce! Charlotte suddenly felt as if she were starving, and hurried home as fast as she could manage in the deep snow.

She intended to go right into the house for a quick snack before starting on the snowman, but when she arrived at the front door, she heard what seemed to be a noisy convention of people gathered in the garden, and she went around the house to investigate. Liu, Coolie, Dossafoo, and Amah Cho Mei were all out there. And so were Dusty, barking furiously, and Jamey, dancing around and helping them build a snowman, now almost finished.

But this snowman wasn't like any Charlotte had ever seen. It was a mammoth Chinese Buddha just like one they had once seen in a temple, a great white mountain rising up from the snow. The servants must have worked all afternoon to build him. He was immense, almost twice as tall as Charlotte, looming over the whole garden with his round bald head, huge bare stomach bulging over his crossed legs, and a benign smile on his face. Liu, Coolie, Dossafoo, and Amah, in their dark padded robes and jackets, dipping up and down to get handfuls of snow to slap on the Buddha, looked like a gathering of happy seals around him, laughing and giggling as if they were no older than Jamey.

"Charlie, come see! Come see!" Jamey plummeted

114

toward Charlotte with Dusty barking at his heels. Forgetting her need for a snack, Charlotte dumped her books right on the snow and joined in with the rest, grabbing handfuls of snow and smoothing them on the huge body of the snow Buddha.

Gradually the frenzied work slowed down, ending finally when it appeared that there really wasn't much left to be done. They all stood back to admire the Buddha, making loud noises of approval. To Charlotte, he looked absolutely perfect in every detail. But not to Dossafoo, it seemed.

After a hasty conference with Liu, Dossafoo rushed into the house, returning a few minutes later stirring something in a tin measuring cup. With newspaper cut into strips to form a small brush, he began to paint a liquid from the cup over the snow crabapples, the good luck symbol the Buddha held in one hand. The paint was red food coloring, and when Dossafoo had finished, the Buddha appeared to be holding real red crabapples.

Another conference was held, and after it, Liu and Coolie went into the house and returned, this time with buckets filled with water. Together with Dossafoo, they slapped water on the Buddha, rubbing it over his body as if they were basting him with oil. Neither Jamey nor Charlotte had any idea what this was all about. Nor would anyone tell them anything.

When the watering down of the Buddha was completed, they stood around him once again to admire him. Under the darkening sky, the Buddha's great form towered over them like a huge Oriental ghost. The talking and laughter became hushed and quiet.

Then, suddenly, Jamey's thin, piping voice rang out. "Ding hao!" he proclaimed.

It was as if a spell had been broken. Liu, Dossafoo, and Coolie began slapping each other on the back, laughing uproariously at the joke Jamey had made. And Charlotte laughed, too, because without quite understanding why, she knew it was a very good thing that Jamey Barrett, aged five, thought the Chinese snow Buddha was ding hao.

In the morning, Charlotte was awakened once again by Jamey, calling to her from the window in her room.

"Charlie, come see the Buddha! Come see him, quick!"

Sleepily, Charlotte threw back her covers and padded barefoot to the window where Jamey stood.

"Oh, Jamey!" she breathed.

The Buddha had become a mirror of ice, catching the frosty morning sunlight and breaking it into ten thousand sparkling lights. So that was what the water was all about, to turn the snow Buddha into an ice Buddha!

Jamey jumped up and down beside Charlotte, too excited to know quite what to do with himself. "Charlie, let's go out and see him. Let's go now!"

"Let's!" said Charlotte. "Run get dressed, Jamey. We'll go see him before breakfast."

Close up, the Buddha was as beautiful as he had seemed from the upstairs window. His slick, shining body was truly like glass, and it was hard as the thick ice at the pond where they skated. Jamey tried it out with the toe of his boot and discovered that. Then, so did Charlotte. All day they played near the Buddha, climbing up onto his lap, chasing Dusty around him, and even trying to build another small Buddha, only *he* turned out so lumpy and funny looking that they ended up rolling in the snow, laughing hysterically. It wasn't until late afternoon, frozen and tired and happy, that they decided they had had enough and went indoors. Charlotte wanted to go to the kitchen to fix them some hot chocolate, but remembering that her parents were having a dinner party that night, a grown-up birthday party for Cousin Philip, she knew the kitchen would be a busy enough place without her presence, and so she obediently rang for Liu instead. Then she and Jamey collapsed on their stomachs in front of the den fireplace.

Dusty came in with them and nestled beside Charlotte on the floor. She ran his long, silky ears through her fingers, thinking how nice it was to have him curled up beside her. She could love him wholeheartedly now that her parents had done as they'd promised and found Maximilian a home. He had gone to live with, of all people, Aunty Mabel! Aunty Mabel had taken him out of kindness and love for Charlotte, she was told, but when Charlotte found she was expected to dangle off Aunty Mabel's lap and allow herself to be kissed, she was not as grateful as she might have been. But she *was* glad that Maximilian had a warm, comfortable home and that she could now rub Dusty's ears without worrying.

"Tell me a story about the ice Buddha," Jamey demanded.

"Shhhhh!" said Charlotte, putting a finger to her lips.

Christene was settled on the couch, reading, and

had scowled when Charlotte, Jamey, and Dusty came romping into the den. Christene wasn't with Moira that afternoon for a change, because they would be together that night. For the very first time, Christene was being included in one of their parents' grown-up parties, at least for the dinner part, and she'd been allowed to invite Moira. It didn't seem fair that Christene should now be taking over the den when she was being allowed to attend the party that night, but she was reading, and had arrived there first, two important points. Charlotte frowned at Jamey to be still.

"Please," Jamey begged.

"I don't know a story about the ice Buddha yet," said Charlotte.

"Then tell me the story about Old Fish," Jamey pleaded. This was a story Charlotte had made up for Jamey several weeks back when he'd been in bed with a cold.

Charlotte sighed. "Jamey, I've told it to you ten times!"

"I want to hear it again. Please, Charlie!"

Charlotte glanced at Christene, and seeing that her sister seemed to be deep in her book and not paying any further attention to them, she said, "Oh, all right. But I'll have to whisper it."

She sat up, her back toward Christene, crossed her legs, and began her story. Although she hadn't really repeated the story to Jamey ten times, she had certainly told it at least five times, each time making it longer and more elaborate. The story was about a boy named Albert, who went boating on a lily pond and was invited down into the water by an ancient speckled fish with long gray whiskers on his chin and a black satin Chinese cap on his head. There Albert was to help the Emperor and Empress of the Kingdom of the Golden Fish choose a color for the Princess's room.

Normally, Charlotte could tell the story in not much more than five minutes, but today, warm and comfortable in front of the fire, with Dusty snuggled quietly against her and Jamey listening raptly to every word, she went on and on. She listed every jewel and semiprecious stone she could think of when describing the Kingdom of the Golden Fish. She told all about the tiny timid Emperor, the terrible fat Empress, and her equally fat daughter, and she described in horrifying detail the disastrous squabble that ended in a horde of angry fish hurling themselves through the water at Albert.

It was at least twenty minutes later before Charlotte finally said, "So Old Fish got Albert back to the boat just in time. When he scrambled in, he could feel the fish actually biting his ankles. 'Thank you, Old Fish!' Albert shouted into the water. But Old Fish had already disappeared under a lily pad. Albert decided he would never go into a fish kingdom again to give advice. And that's the end of the story."

"And then Albert woke up!" said Jamey.

Charlotte shook her head. "I never said Albert woke up before."

"Oh!"

"Do you want him to wake up, Jamey?"

"No!"

"Well then, he didn't."

"Did the story really happen, Charlie?" Jamey asked.

"Yes," said Charlotte without hesitating a second.

Jamey's eyes widened. "Would it happen to me?"

"It might someday," Charlotte replied.

Jamey rolled over on his back, hugging himself gleefully.

"Charlie!" Christene's voice was sharp. "You shouldn't tell Jamey lies like that. He really believes it!"

Charlotte whirled around. Christene had her book down on her lap and must have been listening the whole time. Charlotte, of course, had forgotten about whispering at the very beginning of the story. She was ready with a sharp reply, but never made it because standing in the doorway behind Christene was Cousin Philip! They hadn't heard the doorbell ring, so he must have come in the back way. He had a habit of doing that. Mrs. Barrett didn't approve, but he did it anyway.

"Well—well—" Charlotte stumbled.

Cousin Philip directed a slow wink at her. "If Charlie says it happened, then it must have happened. I personally don't see what's so fantastic about it. After all"—he winked again at Charlotte—"it *is* a fish story."

Christene's head whipped around at the first word from Cousin Philip. Her face reddened when she saw him. "Yes, but Jamey really believes her," she said, flustered.

Cousin Philip sat on the arm of the couch and grinned at Charlotte. "Well, so do I. It's a pretty good story. Did you make that up, Charlie?"

Charlotte nodded, but before she could say anything, Christene flared out, "It sounds as if she just finished reading *Alice in Wonderland!* Old Fish and the whole royal family sound exactly like *Alice* characters, and the fish chasing Albert is just like all the playing cards chasing Alice. It's not surprising," Christene ended disdainfully. "Charlie's only read the book three times!"

"Three times!" exclaimed Cousin Philip.

"Four," said Charlotte sheepishly.

"It's stupid," Christene said. "She reads things so slowly she practically has them memorized the first time. She *can* read fast," Christene added grudgingly. "She just doesn't like to."

"I don't see why you should read fast unless you don't like something," Charlotte said, jutting out her chin at Christene. "And if you don't like something, I don't see why you should read it at all."

"That's a rather Alicey remark, isn't it?" Cousin Philip said. "But not a bad idea. Maybe if I'd read *Alice* slowly—or for that matter, read it four times—I might remember something more about it than the White Rabbit."

Christene jumped up from the couch, closing her book with a snap. "Well, I don't have time to talk about it. I have to get ready for your party tonight, Cousin Philip."

"Oh?" said Cousin Philip. "Are you girls coming?"

"Moira and *I* are," Christene replied pointedly. "Didn't Mother tell you?"

"No, she didn't."

"Oh," Christene said limply. "Well, we are!" Without even glancing at Charlotte, she flounced out of the room.

"How is it you got left out of this?" Cousin Philip asked Charlotte when Christene had gone.

Charlotte shrugged. "I'm just eleven."

"Well, age before beauty, eh, Jamey?" Cousin Philip rose from the arm of the couch, stretched, yawned, and grinned at Charlotte. "I'm off to the kitchen for a few words with your mother. I'll wave to you through the banisters tonight. Wave back, will you?"

Before Charlotte could puzzle out exactly what he had meant by "age before beauty," or wonder how he'd found out about her peeking through the banisters at cocktail and dinner parties, her cousin had gone.

At a few minutes before eight that night, Charlotte was stationed on the top step of the second landing of the stairway, peering downstairs through the banisters. So far, it had been terribly dull because only two people had arrived for the party—Moira and Christene. Even Mr. and Mrs. Barrett were still upstairs dressing. And all the two girls were doing was sitting on the edge of the couch, trying not to wrinkle their dresses and trying to look dignified and grown-up. Charlotte thought it unbelievably boring.

She had to admit one thing, though. While Moira looked exactly like Moira, no different than usual, Christene looked beautiful. Charlotte was really rather proud of the way her sister looked. As the girls had stepped daintily around Charlotte on the stairs, she had seen that Christene's eyes were sparkling, a brighter, clearer blue, it seemed, than they'd ever been. And although Christene had been allowed by her mother to wear pale pink Tangee lipstick, her cheeks didn't need any color. They were a deep pink naturally, from the excitement. Her hair, rinsed in lemon, was almost golden, piled on her head in deep waves. In her new blue velvet dress, she looked beautiful. Yes, thought Charlotte, that was the only word for her.

Charlotte was such a fixture on the landing when there were parties that her parents hardly noticed having to step around her as they swept past at the first ring of the doorbell. Her father stopped adjusting a cuff link just long enough to pat her on the head, and that was all. Then the guests began coming in.

Charlotte always loved to watch guests arrive at a party—the men in their dinner jackets, the ladies in their silk or velvet or lace party dresses, and particularly the Chinese ladies in their slender silk brocade gowns. But tonight the guest Charlotte waited for most anxiously was Cousin Philip, because he had promised to wave to her, and she had promised to wave back.

When he did arrive, finally, he'd brought a most surprising person with him. Charlotte nearly jammed her neck between the railings to get a closer look. She'd been right the first guess—it was Miss Bell! Only this Miss Bell wasn't either one of the two people Charlotte already knew—Miss Dumpymouse of aboard ship a year ago, or Miss Bell of the starched white classroom shirtwaists and the stern dark skirts. This Miss Bell was soft and fluffy in a swirling pink chiffon dress, her bare arms and neck powdery smooth in the dim party lights, and her hair, golden as Christene's, piled, too, into soft curls on top of her head instead of lying in a flat bun on the nape of her neck as it usually did.

In the small American community in Tientsin, where almost everyone knew everyone else, it wasn't surprising that Cousin Philip should have met Miss Bell, but for a moment Charlotte felt confused and betrayed. When she saw Cousin Philip whisper to Miss Bell, then both of them turn toward the stairs and wave, she considered briefly not waving back. But she finally shoved her hand between the railings and gave a quick, short wave in return, feeling herself grow hot as she did.

Then she turned her attention quickly to the expressions on the faces of Moira and Christene as they watched Cousin Philip walk across the room with Miss Bell on his arm. Charlotte felt like giggling as she watched the girls standing around forlornly holding their glasses filled with grape juice, trying to act as if they were having a marvelous time.

She kept her nose pressed to the railing until everyone went in to dinner before she crept up to her room to bed. But once there, she couldn't get to sleep and lay on her back with her eyes open, listening to the party sounds drifting up the stairs to her room. Even with the door closed, she could hear the murmur of voices and bursts of laughter. Then, in the darkness of the room that had once been Christene's and her playroom, she began thinking of how beautiful her sister looked that evening, and how excited about her first grown-up party. She knew now that she hadn't really enjoyed seeing the strained look on Christene's face, and she hoped her sister would end up having the best time she'd ever had in her life.

Charlotte's thoughts about Cousin Philip and Miss Bell weren't so easy to dismiss. She couldn't understand why it was so disturbing to have seen them together, to discover that two people might have private lives apart from her own. She wondered if she liked their knowing one another, and if she ought to be distant and cool and not so tail-waggingly friendly the next time she saw them.

Then she couldn't help remembering how Cousin Philip had stood up for her against Christene that afternoon, how Miss Bell had arranged for her and Anna to spend their recesses together, and how the two of them had waved to her as she peeked through the banisters. Despite the way she'd felt at first, she really liked having them smile at her and wave. They were her two very good friends. And what was wrong, Charlotte asked herself, with her good friends being friends with each other? Nothing that she could see now. It was nice, Charlotte repeated to herself drowsily as she drifted off to sleep at last. It probably was very, very nice!

TEN

CHINESE New Year's always seemed to creep up from nowhere, surprising Charlotte with its sudden arrival. This was partly because the date was different each year, determined by the lunar calendar, which she never could quite understand. But it was also because, as a purely Chinese holiday, it wasn't celebrated either by her family or by her school in any special way. There were no great preparations for it as with Christmas or their own New Year's, so there wasn't much need to announce its approach. Then, suddenly, early one morning or late one night or perhaps even during the day at school, BANG! BANG! BANG, BANG, BANG! The long strings of slim red firecrackers would begin to explode, and Charlotte would know that Chinese New Year's had arrived. That was the way it was each year.

Charlotte loved Chinese New Year's. Even though you didn't really take part in it, you could see it, you could hear it, you could feel it. In their own house, the servants stayed up all of Chinese New Year's Eve, making the bao chiao-tzes that they would eat during the following days of the celebration. The delicious smell of these dough-wrapped meatballs boiling in huge cauldrons on the servants' basement stove carried through the whole house. Then the policeman on the corner would come in to pay his respects to the servants and share in their feast. The sharp sounds of fireworks exploded in their garden as Coolie, for Jamey's benefit, set off with a smoldering joss stick the strings of fire-crackers that hung like long, dangling red insects from their acacia tree.

The complaint Charlotte had about Chinese New Year's was that in the streets near where they lived, nothing much happened. From the sounds she heard, Charlotte was certain that things must be much more exciting in other parts of the city. Since there was so little going on near their house, she couldn't understand why her mother should worry about what might happen to them on the streets. She was furious when on a Saturday afternoon during the New Year's celebration she and Jamey had to be accompanied by Amah Cho Mei when they went to see a Tarzan movie at the nearby Capitol Theatre.

Charlotte was unhappy about having to go to the movies with Jamey in the first place. She usually went with Christene and Moira. Not that this was so wonderful either. Christene was ordered to take her, so she was just a tagalong. Still, tagging along to the movies with Christene and Moira was a lot more respectable than going with Jamey and Amah.

Charlotte didn't like Moira, but she envied Christene anyway for having someone who was a full-time, Saturday-and-Sunday, out-of-school friend. Friday before last, Christene had spent the night with Moira. The Sunday before, they'd gone ice skating together. Today they were practicing their duet for the piano recital, later going to a dinner party at the home of an eighth grade boy, and then all of them going to see Tarzan at *night!*

Why, Charlotte asked herself, did Anna have to be just a school-time, twenty-minute-a-day, recess friend? Why couldn't the two of them be going to the movies together that afternoon? And as if not being with a friend her own age wasn't bad enough, Charlotte had to have Amah dragging along. How embarrassing if she ran into someone from school! Didn't her mother think she was old enough, responsible enough, to look after Jamey?

The whole city was having a good time. Christene, particularly, was having a glorious time. Charlotte was walking tamely to the movies with Jamey and Amah. Normally, Charlotte would have been thrilled about seeing a Tarzan movie. Today, there had to be something more.

"Jamey, guess what I did!" Charlotte said. They were sitting in the front row of the balcony waiting for the movie to begin.

Busy fishing a chocolate-covered peppermint from a small cardboard box, Jamey shook his head.

"Well, you know Amah is supposed to come back to get us after the movie, don't you?"

"Yes," said Jamey, licking his fingers.

"And you remember when I went to ask the ticket man what time the movie ended so I could tell Amah?"

Jamey nodded.

"Well, it ends at four, but I told Amah five! What do you think of that?"

Jamey just looked blank.

Charlotte gave an exasperated sigh. "Jamey, it means that after the movie we can do what we want for a whole hour! What would you like to do?"

Jamey thought this over. "Go across the street and get an ice cream cone."

"What else? Can't you think of anything else?"

"No."

"Well, I can!" said Charlotte. "How would you like to go into Chinese City with me, Jamey? See all the fireworks up close and things like that?"

"No Amah?" asked Jamey.

"No Amah!"

Jamey dived into his box of peppermints again, and after stuffing two of them into his mouth, gave Charlotte a chocolatey grin and nodded.

Charlotte didn't grin back because, after all, she was the grown-up in charge. Sedately, she opened her own box of peppermints. "Then we will," she said. "Now we'll be still because the movie's starting."

The asbestos screen, splashed over with ads for Tiger Balm Ointment and a forthcoming Shirley Temple movie, rose slowly; the heavy blue velvet curtains parted; and for two hours, Charlotte and Jamey were lost in the newsreel, the Mickey Mouse cartoon, and at last, the Tarzan movie itself.

Charlotte felt faraway, dreamy, and strange when she and Jamey stumbled out of the theatre at four o'clock. This was the way she always felt after a movie, wanting to turn around and go right back into the theatre instead of going home where everything was flat and ordinary. Lost in the final exciting moments of the story, she forgot for a few minutes that their own private adventure lay ahead. Then she grabbed Jamey's hand, and they crossed the street to the German confectioner's.

Five minutes flew by easily as they stood before the sparkling glass counter, trying to choose from a tantalizing assortment of candies—marzipan, Jordan almonds, and swirling chocolates—and trays of flaky pastries. They each chose a tiny cherry cream cake frosted with pale green icing to look like a frog's head. Still gazing into the counter, they nibbled the cakes slowly. Then Charlotte bought them each a double-scoop chocolate ice cream cone, and they finally left the sweet shop. Licking their cones intently, they strolled down the street.

When they came to the shops, they stopped to look at ice skates in a window of the English department store, and a display of tiny carved crystal and ivory animals in the windows of a Japanese gift shop. Then Jamey wanted to stop and stare at an old Chinese beggar woman and a small boy sitting on a street corner and holding out rice bowls for money. The boy had only stumps for legs. The hand that held out the bowl was twisted entirely around, and his face was so scarred it looked like the shriveled face of a monkey rather than a boy. The two were professional beggars, Charlotte knew, members of the Beggar Kingdom. The little boy had been maimed, perhaps by his own father, to draw pity. Though the Barrett children had been taught to pay no attention to professional beggars, Charlotte still wished she hadn't spent all her money at the sweet shop, and had a copper or two left in her coat pocket. She took Jamey's hand and pulled him away quickly.

But the ugly, pitiful sight of the beggars seemed to take the spark from their adventure. They walked block after block, their cones long gone. It was getting harder to thread their way through the thickening holiday crowds, and the stone bridge that Charlotte thought would lead them into Chinese City was nowhere in sight. Jamey began to whine about being tired.

Then all at once the bridge rose up ahead of them.

"There, you see, Jamey? It's the bridge, just as I said," Charlotte said triumphantly. Clutching Jamey's hand more tightly, she pushed her way toward the bridge.

Then, hugging the safety of the railing, she stood for a moment with Jamey, looking at the houses reaching down the icy banks of the creek, watching the people in their bright New Year's finery jostling each other on the bridge, seeing the puffs of smoke burst up like dusky mushrooms over the city, followed by the sharp BANG! BANG, BANG, BANG! of the firecrackers that had made them. There it all was, Charlotte told herself, waiting for her—the rows of tiled roofs with their turned-up corners, the candied crabapples and the bright red lacquered ducks hanging in the open shops— all the excitement of Chinese New Year's.

But suddenly the noises seemed deafening. They

were being packed into a crowd of jostling bodies and were hardly able to move. Jamey began to whimper with fright.

This was not a Tarzan adventure where, despite thundering herds of elephants, roaring lions, and evil villains, you could be certain that everything would turn out all right. Nor was it a story where Charlotte could get Albert back in his boat, safe from the hordes of angry fish, and say, "That's the end of the story, Jamey!" This was real, and there was no way to tell how it would end.

"Come on, Jamey," Charlotte said. "We've seen enough. We'll go home now." She tried to keep her voice from trembling.

They managed to push away from the bridge railing. And then suddenly Jamey gave a piercing scream of terror.

Directly in their path, towering over them, was a monstrous red-and-gold paper dragon with terrible glaring eyes, the head of a wild, raucous New Year's parade. The men inside the dragon bucked and pawed the ground, weaving back and forth with howls of make-believe rage, unknowingly forcing Charlotte and Jamey ahead of them, up, up the bridge to the top, then down the other side, pushing them into an almost solid wall of people jamming the main street of Chinese City. Some gyrating young men in the parade surged ahead of the dragon, forcing a path through the crowds so the dragon could move along. Laughing, shouting, strutting about full of importance that they were part of this spectacle, none of the men seemed to notice, or even to see, Charlotte and Jamey. And with the earsplitting

noise of firecrackers shooting off all around them, no one could hear Jamey screaming.

Charlotte wanted to scream, too, but she didn't. All she did was make herself think, Hang on to Jamey! I have to hang on to Jamey! And somehow she did. Packed so tightly into the crowd that she could barely see the sky above, sometimes having her nose pressed into someone's padded jacket ahead of her so she couldn't breathe, sometimes holding her breath because it kept her from screaming, feeling certain that Jamey would be torn away from her at any moment because her arm and hand ached so that she could hardly bear it, somehow she *did* hold on to him.

Please make this a bad dream! Please make it only a terrible story! Please let me say, "And that's the end of the story," and have it *be* the end! And please let Jamey and me be back in our own house! Oh, please!

The words ran through Charlotte's head like a chant, over and over, as they were pushed and pulled ahead of the dragon parade, thrust deeper and deeper into the heart of Chinese City until Charlotte lost all track of where they were. And then suddenly Charlotte found herself being gradually shoved to one side of the street and, still holding on to Jamey, almost catapulted through a door into the dimness of a large room. Although there were five or six Chinese people in the room, it seemed strangely quiet after the terrible racket in the street. One look at the counters and shelves that lined the room, and Charlotte knew that they had entered some kind of shop.

The shock of being practically thrown into the shop had stopped Jamey's crying for a moment, but as soon as he saw that this wasn't home and there was nothing familiar about it, he began to sob again. The people in the shop had stopped talking when Charlotte and Jamey appeared, and were now watching them curiously.

"Please, Jamey! You have to stop crying," Charlotte pleaded, though she felt as if she were going to cry herself. "Look! Here's a counter with candy, just like the sweet seller. Come see it, Jamey."

Charlotte pulled him to one side of the shop, but he wouldn't be distracted by anything she pointed out to him, and he continued to sob. Charlotte looked around desperately at the strange faces staring at them. Why didn't someone see that they were in trouble and needed help? Couldn't someone come over and try to talk to them?

One of the staring faces belonged to a very old man who stood behind the counter at the back of the shop. Next to him stood a small boy whose head barely reached over the top of the counter, and who kept pulling at the old man's cotton gown and pointing at Charlotte and Jamey. The old man finally seemed to come to life. Leaning over, he whispered something to the boy, gesturing excitedly and pointing first to Charlotte and Jamey, then out the back door of the shop. At first the boy didn't move, too busy watching the strange boy and girl, but the old man gave him a firm push, and he flew through the back door. The old man then hurried around the counter where Charlotte stood with the hysterical Jamey. For a moment, he simply remained standing there, his hands folded over his stomach, his head tilted, watching them.

Then his head began to bob up and down, and he smiled at Charlotte. "Ah! Ah!" he said, and holding a finger up as if to show her he had finally thought of something, he scurried around behind the counter once more. Charlotte watched him curiously as he lifted the glass lid of the counter, reached in, and drew out a large stick of sesame candy. He held it up, showing it to Charlotte, then pulled from under the counter a small square of red paper. He folded this into a cone and dropped the sesame candy into it. Then he came from behind the counter, handing the paper cone to Charlotte, and at the same time pointing to Jamey as if to say, "Give it to him."

Charlotte didn't know what to do. Should Jamey have candy that had been lying unwrapped in a store in Chinese City, that hadn't come in a bottle or tin from their own compradore, the German confectioner's, or their own kitchen? And did the old shopkeeper expect her to buy the candy? Charlotte couldn't. She had no money left, not one copper!

But the old man kept pushing the paper cone toward her and smiling, and she knew finally that he wasn't trying to sell it to her at all. He wanted to give it to her for Jamey. And it would be a terrible insult if she refused.

Hesitantly, Charlotte held out her hand and took the candy in the red cone. "Sheh sheh," she said.

"Ah-h-h! Jungo hwa!" the old man said, clapping his hands together and smiling at the other people in his shop.

"Jungo hwa! Jungo hwa!" The murmur rose in the

shop. All the staring, stony faces were now smiling at each other, nodding and saying, "Jungo hwa!"

"Talk Chinese! Talk Chinese!" is what they were saying. They hadn't been cold and unfeeling before. They had only been perplexed and a little shy of these two strange foreign children who had suddenly materialized in a shop in the middle of Chinese City. As if they had been statues given life by two magic words, they now clustered around Charlotte and Jamey. He had quieted down as soon as the exciting red paper cone had reached his hands, and he was now sucking happily on the stick of sesame candy.

"Ah! Ah!" the Chinese all said, nodding as Jamey smiled shyly up at them through tear-filled eyes. Several of them reached out and patted him kindly on the head.

Then the torrent of Chinese began, everyone talking at once and much too fast. Charlotte's Chinese wasn't nearly good enough to keep up with all of it, or even any of it. All she could do was stand shaking her head to show she didn't understand them.

She knew they must be asking her questions, but what questions? One question must surely have been how they'd come to be there. That one Charlotte couldn't possibly answer in Chinese. But she also guessed that they must be asking where she and Jamey lived, and that question she could answer.

"Newchwang Loo," Charlotte said. "Newchwang Loo," she repeated slowly and clearly.

The rattling conversation came to a stop. "Newchwang Loo?" A dismayed silence fell over the shop as everyone looked at everyone else questioningly and finally realized that no one there had heard of Newchwang Loo.

The shopkeeper shook his head. "Ai ya! Mayo fadze!" There was no help for it!

The hubbub started up again and sounded as if it might go on indefinitely. But in a moment the small boy returned, bringing with him an older boy about thirteen or fourteen, who wore the cap and uniform of a Chinese student. The old man took the boy by the arm and, as he pelted him with explanations, drew him toward Charlotte and Jamey.

The boy looked shyly at Charlotte and said very slowly and carefully, "Grandfather says you are English boy and girl. You are lost?"

"Oh, yes!" Charlotte cried. "We're not English. We're American, but we *are* lost. Please, can you help us to get home?"

"Where do you live?" the boy asked.

"Across the bridge. Newchwang Loo," Charlotte replied promptly.

The boy shook his head, puzzled. With much waving of arms and pointing, he spoke again to his grandfather.

Then smiling, he said to Charlotte, "I can help you. Please, come with me. We find help." He beckoned to Charlotte, at the same time moving toward the back door.

Charlotte quickly picked up Jamey's free hand, the one that wasn't clutching the red paper cone, and followed him. When she reached the door, she turned back. She wanted to say something to these strangers

138

who had become friends, to the wonderful shopkeeper who had helped them. But what could she do or say? As she hesitated, Jamey tugged impatiently at her hand.

"Jamey, just a minute. I'm coming."

To Charlotte's surprise, Jamey thrust the remains of the crumpled red paper into her hand. Then, facing the small audience before him, he put his hands together, tips of fingers to his chin in the position of respect, and made a deep bow. "Sheh sheh!" he said. Then he faced the old shopkeeper and bowed again. "Sheh sheh, lao shen shung!" Thank you, venerable sir!

The shop rang with clapping, laughter, and loud noises of approval, while the old shopkeeper beamed. He had been given much "face" by what Jamey had said, much prestige with his customers. Jamey had succeeded once again in giving the very best thank-you anybody could have given. Charlotte could hardly believe that her little brother, crying like a baby only minutes ago, had known how to do something so grownup, so absolutely proper and right. She was very proud of him. Now she could leave happily, knowing that something hadn't been left undone or unsaid. Waving to everyone in the shop, Charlotte and Jamey went out the back door to where the young student stood waiting for them.

Charlotte hated to think that they would have to go back into the crowds and noise of the main streets of Chinese City, but the boy never took them there. Up a quiet back alley, down a side street, up another alley they went until Charlotte felt the boy himself was lost. Even though he kept smiling back at them encouragingly, she couldn't help being frightened. She nearly cried with joy and relief when the boy stopped at last before a small gate set deep in a wall, and she read the words painted on a wooden plaque that hung beside the gate—American Presbyterian Mission!

The boy pushed a button in the wall, and they could hear a bell ring faintly somewhere within. In a few moments, a gray-coated servant came to the door. The student held a swift conversation with him, then said to Charlotte and Jamey, "Go with him. He will take you to people to help you."

"Oh, aren't you coming with us?" Charlotte asked, thinking that this kind boy should surely come inside to be thanked by the people in the mission.

"No. Not needed," the boy said. "You go." He motioned his head toward the servant.

Almost unconsciously, Charlotte held out her hand. The young student looked at it hesitantly, as if the act puzzled him; then, smiling, he took it, and he and Charlotte shook hands. "Thank you," Charlotte said.

The boy smiled again, then turned and ran swiftly to the corner and disappeared.

Silently, Charlotte and Jamey followed the servant through the courtyard, through the entryway of the house, and into a living room, where two boys lay on their stomachs in front of the fireplace playing checkers. The boys looked up as Charlotte and Jamey came into the room. They were Skinny Buttrick and Barry Dameron!

For a time after that, everything seemed a happy blur in Charlotte's mind—meeting Skinny's parents, Dr. and Mrs. Buttrick; being told what a brave girl she was; finding out that the young student who had helped them was Chi Chien Hsu, who had once taken English lessons from Dr. Buttrick; and finally being escorted home in a rickshaw by Dr. Buttrick.

But the happy blur ended when at last the rickshaw stopped in front of their home and Charlotte, Dr. Buttrick, and Jamey went into the house. Charlotte saw Amah Cho Mei huddled in a chair in the living room, moaning and weeping into the sleeve of her familiar white jacket, while her father, his face gray and drawn, spoke to a policeman, and her mother sat on the couch with her arm tightly wrapped around Christene.

The terror of the adventure was over for Jamey. He'd been given a stick of sesame candy by a kind old Chinese man. He'd done something splendid and been given a round of applause in the shop. He'd been fed cocoa and cookies and had a huge fuss made over him by Dr. and Mrs. Buttrick. Now he was home again, and everything was just as it had always been. He beamed at his assembled family and raced toward his mother to begin telling about the exciting day he'd had.

Charlotte remained standing in the doorway, unable to move. She began to tremble violently, and tears came into her eyes, but still she couldn't move. Then, at last, her father held out his arms to her, and she ran into them, sobbing.

ELEVEN

"WELL, taking Jamey and going off to Chinese City during the New Year's holiday really was a childish thing to do, Charlotte!" said Christene the next day, furious because she'd now be stuck with Charlotte on Saturday afternoons. "No wonder Mother sent Amah with you to the movies. You were lucky. I'd have sent a police dog! It's a wonder Mother and Daddy didn't murder you when you got home."

"It wasn't childish! It was an accident. I didn't mean to," Charlotte threw back at Christene, knowing that these rebuttals didn't make any sense and were lies as well.

Christene replied to this with an icy stare.

Although Charlotte felt forced to put up a defense with Christene, she agreed with her completely. She still couldn't believe that all she'd gotten as punishment was a serious talk from her father. He'd said that he and her mother thought the outcome of the adventure was punishment enough. And it was; Charlotte knew she would never forget the looks on her parents' faces when she had walked through the door with Dr. Buttrick and Jamey.

Still, she couldn't help thinking how unfair it had all been. If she'd had a friend, a *real* friend, none of it would have happened. It wasn't fair that the only friend she had was someone whose father placed impossible restrictions on their being friends at all, even at school. But Anna thought her father was right in what he did, so how could she, Charlotte, persuade Anna to talk to her father and make him see that they needed to be friends outside of school? How could she make their friendship so important that Anna would even want to ask?

And then Charlotte began thinking about Beverly Showberg and her "momentos."

Beverly and her mother and father had moved into the apartment building in Los Angeles where the Barretts had lived shortly before returning to China. Mrs. Showberg wanted Beverly to be a movie star, so she had bleached Beverly's hair blond, put it in corkscrew curls all over her head, and frequently took her by bus into Hollywood, where she paraded her up and down Hollywood Boulevard hoping that someone would discover her for the movies. This had seemed a bit ridiculous to Charlotte, since Beverly was already beginning to be string beany and had teeth that stuck out almost as far as her own. But Charlotte had to admit that in spite of herself, back in Los Angeles she'd been impressed with Beverly.

One thing Charlotte never understood was why such an impressive person as Beverly Showberg wasn't surrounded by dozens of friends, since she'd moved from an apartment only three blocks away. But Charlotte was certain Beverly had friends because her room was filled with mementos (only Beverly called them "momentos") from all of them. Boys did ugly things like pricking their fingers and exchanging drops of blood to insure undying friendship, Beverly had explained to Charlotte, but exchanging "momentos" was what girls did. She had shown Charlotte a ring featuring, according to Beverly, a real "carrot" diamond that looked more like glass to Charlotte though she never said so, a brass pillbox, a Japanese silk handkerchief, a barrette with a glass angel on it, and a number of other things given to her by Margie, Helene, Billie, Shirley, and a string of other girls.

Charlotte was awestruck by all this and rather overwhelmed when Beverly sprung open her big blue eyes one day soon after they'd met and said that *they* should exchange "momentos." In the end, though, Charlotte was glad she'd had to leave for China before they got around to exchanging anything, because deep down inside, secretly, she wasn't sure she wanted Beverly for an undying friend. But the idea of giving and receiving a memento, as an exciting, wonderful, special thing you did with a friend, had remained with her ever since.

Now Charlotte decided that she would tell Anna

about the idea to see what Anna thought of it, to see if Anna cared enough to want to exchange mementos with her. If she did, wouldn't that prove something? Charlotte could hardly wait until recess the next morning to speak to Anna.

"Anna," Charlotte said, carelessly studying the thumb of her red woolen glove, "would you like me to tell you about this friend of mine in Los Angeles?" They were strolling together at the lower end of the playground, protected by the high wall from the icy winds off the river. Charlotte had spent the entire hour and a half until recess daydreaming in class, trying to think of the best way to present the idea to Anna. She had settled, finally, on a roundabout way so that if Anna didn't like the idea, it would be less embarrassing for both of them.

Anna looked at her in surprise. "But, Charlie, you once told me that you did not have a special friend in America."

"Oh, she wasn't a special friend," Charlotte said quickly. "She was—she was just someone I met." Then, feeling that she ought to say something more impressive than that, she added limply, "She's sort of—in the movies."

"In the movies!" Anna's eyes were sparkling. But a moment later she shook her head strangely and stared at the ground.

"What's wrong, Anna?" Charlotte asked.

"Nothing! Oh, I am so sorry, Charlie." Anna paused and then blurted out, "It is just that I am not allowed to go to the movies, and I should not— It is that—" She stopped in confusion.

"You mean you've never been?" asked Charlotte. Later, when she thought about it, it did seem strange that she and Anna had never discussed going to the movies, but they hadn't. She had just supposed that Anna went like everyone else.

"I have been once," Anna said as if she should be apologizing for it. "William and I were taken to see Shirley Temple by friends of our family, but they had forgotten to ask the permission of our father. He did not complain to our friends because that would not have been polite, but William and I cannot go again. My father does not like the movies." Anna paused, then turned eagerly once more to Charlotte. Her eyes were sparkling again. "Oh, Charlie, is this someone you know what you call a movie star?"

Charlotte hadn't intended to lie about Beverly. It was a kind of accident. But as long as the words were out and Anna was so excited about it, what difference did it really make? Charlotte had said "sort of in the movies," which didn't make it an out-and-out lie, and for all she knew, Beverly might be in the movies by now. So why not go ahead with it? It did sound glamorous and thrilling, and it would certainly make the idea of mementos seem much more important.

"Well, she isn't a big star or anything like that, or at least she wasn't *then*," said Charlotte, intimating that things might be different *now*.

"Is she pretty?" Anna asked breathlessly.

"Oh yes," said Charlotte. "She has—oh, the most

beautiful great big blue eyes, and yellow curls all over her head!"

"Just like Shirley Temple?" Anna asked.

"Just like that!" Charlotte said. "And she tap dances, too, just like Shirley." When Beverly had demonstrated her tap dancing ability in front of their apartment house, Charlotte had thought that with her skinny arms and legs flying around, she'd looked like a grasshopper. But now, over a year later, encouraged by Anna's rapt attention, she could almost believe all these wonderful things, and so she went on and on describing all of Beverly's starlike qualities.

Recess was almost over before Charlotte arrived at the most important point about Beverly—her dozens and dozens of friends. Charlotte explained that she had never seen any of them, but had only seen the mementos Beverly and her friends had exchanged. And didn't Anna think exchanging mementos the most beautiful idea in the whole world? asked Charlotte.

Anna merely looked puzzled. "I do not think I understand what it is—exchanging these me—me—"

"Mementos," Charlotte said. "Gifts, Anna. Do you remember when Miss Bell read the class the chapter from that book *Tom Sawyer?*"

Anna nodded.

"Well, do you remember where Tom and his friend Huckleberry exchanged drops of blood to show what good friends they were?"

"Yes," said Anna.

"Well, *Beverly* told me that *girls* exchange gifts when they want to seal their friendship. Anna, don't you think that's the most beautiful idea?" Charlotte repeated.

For a few moments, as Charlotte waited anxiously for a reply, Anna said nothing.

"Anna?" said Charlotte.

Anna started. "I am sorry, Charlie. I did not mean to be rude. Yes, it is a most beautiful idea, but I was thinking. Did you exchange this—this memento with Beverly?"

"Oh no!" Charlotte replied quickly. "I told you, Anna, that I didn't know her very well. We just met, that's all. You only do that with *special* friends."

A few more anxious moments passed for Charlotte, and then Anna said, "*We* are special friends?"

"You are *my* special friend," said Charlotte.

"And you are mine," said Anna.

A sudden, swift shyness came over them, and neither could say anything. They walked along the playground wall in silence. Then Charlotte looked at Anna, and Anna looked back at Charlotte. They smiled, and then at the same instant, both threw their hands over their mouths and giggled into them like two silly first graders! And that was the way they felt, silly and giggly and wonderful because they'd just found out this marvelous thing about each other. They were each other's special friend!

"Shall we then exchange these—these mementos?" Anna asked.

"Oh yes!" Charlotte said, and they both giggled into their hands again because it seemed the best way to express their joy at this miraculous event.

"Tomorrow!" Charlotte sang out. "Let's do it tomorrow!"

Anna frowned slightly. "Oh, Charlie, for such an important thing as exchanging me-men-tos with a special friend, should we not take longer? I should like to have more days to think about what I shall give you. Could we do this next—a week from next Friday, perhaps?"

Tomorrow! Next week! Friday of next week! What difference did it make? They were going to exchange gifts to seal their friendship. What difference did it make what day it happened, as long as it happened?

TWELVE

NOW there remained the big decision to make—what to give Anna? Charlotte lost all count of how many times she dumped the contents of her treasure box onto her bed to sort hopelessly through them. She and Anna had agreed that they should give each other something they already owned, but now Charlotte wondered if this was such a good idea. The things in her treasure box were all terribly precious to *her*, but how precious would they be to Anna? For instance, would Anna, nearly two years older than she was, be interested in a tiny celluloid doll resting in a matchbox bed made by an early amah for Charlotte when she'd had the chicken pox? And what would Anna possibly think of a gift of three agate marbles, a tiny muslin sack filled with used postage stamps, or an empty aspirin tin decorated by Charlotte with red nail polish?

Charlotte lined these and all her other treasures up on her bed and then disconsolately picked up a little unopened glass jar of Bunte's raspberry drops that had come in her Christmas stocking a year before. The once-sparkling drops were now dull and stuck together from having sat in the cupboard through a very hot summer. Charlotte hadn't been able to part with them any more than she'd been able to part with the powder puff from her mother, the shell from Christene, or the bottle top from Dossafoo. Now, of course, she knew she would part with any of these, and a dozen other things, if she thought they would be the right gift for Anna.

Charlotte had pestered her family to death for ideas and, as far as she was concerned, gotten nowhere.

"It's strictly a problem for the ladies," her father said flatly. "If it were up to me, I'd exchange the drops of blood and be done with it."

"Oh, Daddy!" Charlotte said disgustedly.

Her mother's idea, however, wasn't much better. She suggested that Charlotte embroider a handkerchief for Anna.

"Ugh!" said Charlotte, certain that the only good thing about a handkerchief embroidered by herself would be that you wouldn't mind blowing your nose into it.

"Why don't you give her a book?" Christene said when Charlotte questioned her. She was in a very light-hearted mood because Mrs. Barrett had said she might wear pink nail polish to Moira's party, and she was happily getting her fingernails ready to apply it.

"Chrissy, I can't," Charlotte wailed. "All my books are signed in by people who've given them to me. You can't give away a gift like that"—Charlotte stopped a moment—"can you?"

"Probably not," said Christene. She studied her

fingernails carefully, then looked up to see Charlotte still there. "Well, write one, why don't you?" she said blithely.

"Oh, Chris!" said Charlotte. She watched Christene carefully lift the little brush from the bottle of polish and, biting her lip, apply the first drop to a fingernail. Knowing better than to disturb her sister further at this delicate moment, Charlotte quietly left.

Write a book. Write a book. It was a stupid idea and Christene was, of course, just teasing her, but still the idea kept running through her head. Write a book? No, but why not *make* a book? A scrapbook! Charlotte and Anna had agreed that they should only give something they already had. They weren't to go out and buy anything. But what was wrong with *making* the gift from things you already had—construction paper, cardboard, paint, paste, and, most important of all, pictures. The pictures would come from the magazines that were sent to them from America, pictures showing Anna all the things Charlotte had only been telling her about.

And while Charlotte was thinking over what special kinds of pictures Anna would most like to see, she began to remember the sparkling look in Anna's eyes when they'd talked about Beverly, the eager questions she'd asked. And more than anything, she remembered the sound of Anna's voice when she said her father would not allow her to go to the movies again. So, thought Charlotte finally, Anna couldn't go to the movies? Well then, she would bring the movies to Anna—in a scrapbook! She and Anna might never be able to go to a Saturday matinee together, but together they would go on a tour of a scrapbook filled with pictures of movie stars.

The next morning, Saturday, Charlotte was up even before she heard the sounds of Dossafoo rattling pans on the iron stove. And even before she was summoned to breakfast by Liu, she was already seated at the old play table in what was now her bedroom, surrounded by construction paper, a large jar of Carter's paste, scissors, pencils, ruler, and a Pink Pearl eraser—Charlotte was never certain that she wouldn't need to rub out something. She was blissfully cutting out pictures from a movie magazine, with at least a dozen others piled in front of her.

Charlotte actually had only a few movie magazines of her own, dog-eared and thumbed through, but still perfectly good as sources of pictures for the scrapbook. But the big surprise had been Christene's willingness to give up some of *hers*, even some of her favorite *Photoplays*. Christene and Moira poured over these magazines for hours on end, and Charlotte couldn't believe her luck when Christene, without any argument, agreed to let her cut up some of her older ones.

This was, Christene said, probably the most organized thing Charlotte had ever done in her life. Charlotte was slightly annoyed by this remark, but had to agree that it might be true. Besides the construction paper, paste, and other necessary items, she had rounded up as many boxes as she could find—two stationery boxes, her treasure box (emptied for the occasion), a cracker tin, a biscuit tin, three shoe boxes loaned by her father, and several other assorted containers. These containers, separated so she could use both the box and its lid, were set in a circle around her chair, and into them she was making separate piles of Errol Flynn, Ginger Rogers, William Powell, and all the stars. Each star would have his own separate section in the book, and even particular colors. Orange, black, and blue construction paper was for the men; red, green, and yellow for the ladies. Pink was reserved for Shirley Temple, brown for Rin Tin Tin, the dog movie star, and lavender for Anna May Wong. Charlotte couldn't help wondering what Anna would say when she came to the lavender pages. Anna probably didn't even know there was a Chinese movie star, Charlotte told herself delightedly.

For two glorious, busy days, Charlotte sat at the play table, cutting and pasting. By Sunday, exhausted but happy, she had all the pages ready for her book, and there was only the cover left to make. Only the cover! But that had to be the most special thing about the scrapbook, because it was the introduction to everything that lay within.

Tired as she was, Charlotte knew that she had to start work on the cover at once. It would have been easy, of course, if she were only going to cover cardboard with construction paper and print letters on it. But she had decided on something much more difficult. She was going to cover cardboard in a scrap of pale blue velveteen, and then embroider in gold the word "Stars" across the top, with gold stars cascading down from it. Luckily, they had someone in their home who did the most beautiful embroidery in the world, someone Charlotte could go to for all the help and instruction she needed.

"Can do," Amah Cho Mei said to Charlotte. "I can make very nice 'broidery. Can finish by end of week."

"No, *I'm* going to do it," said Charlotte firmly.

"Ai ya!" said Amah, who had seen some of Charlotte's earlier work in embroidery. But she picked up her needle, and after sighing and shaking her head a few times to impress Charlotte with what she thought of the whole business, she took a muslin scrap from her sewing basket and patiently taught Charlotte the stitches she would need.

By bedtime Sunday night, Charlotte was ready to burst into tears and scream at the first person who so much as breathed a critical word in her direction. She had embroidered her skirt into the muslin so many times that it looked like a pincushion, and she'd stuck her fingers so often with the needle that she began to agree with her father; it *would* have been easier just to exchange blood drops with Anna and be done with it. But at last, after a careful study of her work and only a few groans and sighs, Amah agreed that the next day after school Charlotte could start on the blue velveteen.

Nobody, especially Charlotte, really thought she would have the scrapbook cover finished on time, or that it would be anything she would be proud to give to Anna. But it was both of those things. Charlotte couldn't get over the spotlessly clean cover (she had washed her hands so many times while working that her skin had nearly peeled off), the shining gold letters marching across the top, and the stars cascading down the velvet. Christene had used the word "dribbling" instead of "cascading," but even she had to admit that the whole effect wasn't bad at all. Mr. and Mrs. Barrett said they thought it was beautiful. Quite modestly, Charlotte did, too. She propped the scrapbook up beside her bed that night so it would be the last thing she saw before she went to sleep and the first thing she would see in the morning.

Somehow Charlotte managed to get to sleep that night and to live until recess the next morning when she and Anna opened their gifts, standing behind the school building where no one could see them.

It was funny how something that they had whispered and giggled about all week could suddenly bring on the most terrible shyness. They actually wasted four whole minutes of recess, shivering in the icy winds that blew around the school building, because neither wanted to open her package first. Finally, they decided to open them together, at the very same moment.

"Oh, Anna!"

"Oh, Charlie!"

They said it together, and then laughed at the way their voices sounded. They looked at one another with shining eyes.

"Oh, Anna, they're beautiful!" Charlotte said, and took from the small green-brocade box Anna had given her a pair of gold earrings with carved jade pendants.

"Do you really like them?" Anna asked anxiously.

"Yes! They're the most beautiful things I've ever seen!" Charlotte exclaimed.

Then, to her surprise, Anna gasped, looked with horror from the earrings Charlotte held in her hand, to her face, to the earrings again.

"Charlie, I do not know why—I did not think to look—oh, Charlie," Anna wailed. "The earrings are for ears that have been pierced! I do not know why I did not think to look at your ears!" Anna, of course, like many Chinese girls, did have her ears pierced and wore small gold loops through them all the time.

"I don't care!" Charlotte said. "It doesn't matter, Anna. I love the earrings, and I wouldn't give them up for anything. Besides, I'll probably have my ears done someday."

She'd actually never had such a thought in her whole life. For that matter, she'd never considered wearing earrings at all, not any kind. But she certainly wasn't going to tell Anna that. Besides, what difference did it make? It had come to her as a surprise that whole week how little she cared what Anna's gift to her would be. All that mattered was that it came from Anna. She would take the earrings, put them immediately into her treasure box, and forever and ever, whenever she looked at them, she would remember Anna. Who cared whether she ever wore them or not?

"Charlie!" Anna cried. "Oh, Charlie, I am so rude. I have said nothing yet about your gift to me. Charlie, it is—it is—" Anna's black almond eyes glowed as she hesitated, trying to find the right words to say. "Charlie, did you make this book for me?" She touched a gold star lightly with her forefinger, then rubbed the silk threads gently as if she needed to make herself believe the book was real.

"Yes." Charlotte nodded shyly as she watched Anna open the velvet cover and read the first page of the scrapbook.

"'Stars, by Charlotte Barrett. To Anna Chung, a memento from her friend Charlotte.'" Anna breathed the words softly, half to herself, half to Charlotte, and then looked up. "Oh, Charlie!"

With just that, Charlotte knew that all her work had been worth it—the punctured fingers, the staying up at night until her eyes blurred, the cutting, the pasting, the worrying. All of it, every bit of it—all worth it!

THIRTEEN

"LOOK, Daddy, look what Anna gave me!" Charlotte came bursting into the den, proudly holding the earrings up to her ears. Her father was there with her mother, having a before-dinner drink.

"Whooee! Pretty grown-up all of a sudden. When are you planning to wear those, young lady?" Mr. Barrett pulled his glasses down to the end of his nose and looked at Charlotte over them, laughing.

Mrs. Barrett firmly snapped off a piece of wool from the red-and-white-striped scarf she was knitting for Jamey. "Not very soon, I hope!" She had seen the earrings earlier when Charlotte came home from school, so she knew about them already.

"I can't wear them anyway," said Charlotte, giggling. "They're for pierced ears. Anna forgot to look at my ears and see they don't have little holes in them."

"Fancy that," said Mr. Barrett.

"It's a funny kind of present for a young girl," Mrs. Barrett said thoughtfully. "But then, as Charlie says, Anna is nearly two years older than she is, and by Chinese custom, I suppose is quite old enough for earrings, even a sophisticated pendant type like these."

"Mother, it's not a funny kind of present," Charlotte said indignantly. "They're beautiful!"

"Of course they are, dear. I never meant to imply that they weren't. Jim"—Mrs. Barrett picked up the knitting from her lap—"take a look at them a minute. I mean, up close. Charlie, let Daddy see the earrings, will you?"

Mr. Barrett took the earrings from Charlotte and studied them closely for a moment. Then he took a sip from his drink and whistled softly. "Good lord, these must have cost a fortune! They're carved from a very fine piece of jade. Looks like a solid gold setting, too."

"My thoughts exactly," Mrs. Barrett said. "I don't see how we can let Charlie accept such an expensive gift. Can you imagine what they'll think when they see her—" She looked up from her knitting, saw Charlotte watching her curiously, and cut off the sentence.

But she hadn't needed to, Charlotte thought. She knew exactly what her mother was going to say. "Can you imagine what they'll think when they see her *scrapbook!*"

Well, what was wrong with the scrapbook? Anna had loved it just as much as Charlotte had loved the earrings. Somehow, the whole thing was getting out of hand, and Charlotte began to wish she had never brought her family into it. Since it was beginning to sound suspiciously as if they might even order her to give the earrings back, she decided she had better leave the room before the conversation reached that point.

"Where are you going?" her father asked, as if her leaving was the biggest surprise of his life.

"To put my earrings away," replied Charlotte loftily.

"Don't you think you'd better let me keep them for you?" her mother asked.

"Why?"

"Well, they'd be much safer if I put them away. You don't want anything to happen to them, do you?"

What kind of stupid question was that? wondered Charlotte. Of course, she didn't want anything to happen to the earrings. Did her mother think she was some kind of infant who couldn't be counted on to take care of them? She intended to put them in her Huntley & Palmer treasure box. She had stored any number of things there for two whole years, and nothing had happened to *them*.

"They'll be perfectly safe with me," said Charlotte with injured dignity, and she thumped out of the room in a huff.

Charlotte felt she could hardly live through the weekend, waiting to get back to school the following week. Anna had promised to bring the scrapbook to school Monday so that Charlotte could take her on a guided tour of the stars.

Racing to school Monday morning, Charlotte was annoyed with Jamey because he dragged his feet and complained of a stomachache. She had to slow down for him finally after they'd crossed the bridge, but dumped him off unceremoniously at the kindergarten building with a firm reminder that he'd be fine just as soon as school started. Then she rushed up the stairs, threw off her coat and tam, raced to her desk, and plopped down in it breathlessly. Miss Bell, busy putting the day's arithmetic problems on the blackboard, looked at her with surprise. But Charlotte was determined to be waiting there to see Anna when she came in, no matter how long or how boring the wait.

She kept hoping that Anna might be even a few seconds early, but promptly three minutes before the bell rang, as usual, Anna and William scurried in. Anna looked strangely pale and drawn. She couldn't miss seeing Charlotte beaming at her from her desk, but she gave only a quick nervous smile in return, slipped into her desk, and began studiedly to arrange the books she'd brought with her in the desk drawer. Among Anna's books, Charlotte saw no pale-blue velvet-covered scrapbook. Her stomach squeezed into a sick tight lump as she suddenly remembered the conversation she'd had with her mother and father about the earrings.

Still, Charlotte asked herself, how could she be certain that their exchange of gifts had anything to do with the way Anna was behaving? Perhaps, like Jamey, she only had a stomachache and had forgotten the scrapbook because she didn't feel well. By the time recess arrived, Charlotte had convinced herself that there was probably a very simple explanation for what was happening. When the bell rang, she flew to Anna's desk.

"Anna, what happened? Where's the book?" Charlotte whispered because there were still other boys and girls in the room, trailing out the door.

For a few uncomfortable moments, Anna stared down at her desk. When she looked up, there were tears trembling on her lashes. "Charlie, I cannot go out with you today. We cannot have lessons at recess together again."

Charlotte's throat suddenly felt tight and dry. "Why, Anna? Why?"

"It is the wish of my father."

"Anna, it's because of the gifts, isn't it? It's because I only gave you a silly old—"

"No! No! Please, Charlie! Please, it is no use to talk about it. It is my father's wish. Now I must speak with Miss Bell. I must give her a letter from my father."

"Anna, if we don't have recess lessons anymore, does it mean that"—Charlotte felt her face grow hot—"that we aren't special friends anymore either?"

"It does not mean such a thing, Charlie!" Anna's voice broke. "For me, you will always be a most special friend! But please now"—her voice became filled with terror—"I must talk to our teacher!" She jumped up from her desk and, with a white rice paper envelope clutched in her hand, walked quickly to Miss Bell's desk.

Miss Bell, who had seemed to be deep in her work of correcting papers, looked up at once. With a puzzled frown, she took the envelope Anna held out to her.

Charlotte ran out the door, heading for the cloakroom. The cloakroom could be an exciting place when you had a friend laughing there with you before you went out to recess, or whispering something to you before you went into class. Somehow, then, you didn't notice how dim and dingy it was, how it smelled of musty wood, wet wool, and stale lunches. Alone, the cloakroom would be the last place in the world you would want to spend twenty minutes of recess. But it just happened to be the only place Charlotte knew where she could stand with her face buried in her coat trying to keep from crying.

"I'm so awfully sorry, Charlie," Miss Bell said simply, after handing Charlotte a handkerchief from the class "spare handkerchief" box on her desk, and waiting patiently for her to blow into it.

It was the end of the school day, probably the longest school day Charlotte had ever spent in her life, and she had been sitting beside Miss Bell's desk, waiting hopefully to be told by the magical Miss Bell that everything would be straightened out, that it was all a mistake. But she heard only what she had heard from Anna, that there would be no more "recess lessons" together.

Miss Bell looked as if she had spent a very long day, too. Her hair stood up in a hump on one side where she'd run her fingers through it. Her glasses were smudged. She had a pencil mark on her chin and red chalk dust from the blackboard across the front of her white blouse. She didn't look crisp or fresh or sparkling as she usually did. She just looked tired.

But the clear blue eyes behind the glasses were warm and sympathetic, and Charlotte, after the brave struggle all day since recess, had given up and embarrassed herself by bursting into tears in front of her teacher. She sniffed miserably, clutching the wet handkerchief on her lap.

"It was because of the presents we gave each other, wasn't it?"

Miss Bell seemed about to say "no," then apparently changed her mind. "Yes, I'm afraid it was."

"Oh, Miss Bell," Charlotte cried. "I'll give the earrings back. I don't want them anymore. I only want Anna!"

"I'm sure you do," Miss Bell said gently. "But the Chinese are very proud people, Charlie. Mr. and Mrs. Chung wouldn't allow Anna to take them back."

"Even if I *want* to give them back?"

"Not even then," said Miss Bell.

"Well—well then, couldn't I give something to make up for the scrapbook—something that—that *costs* a lot?" Considering that all the contents of Charlotte's treasure box, excluding the earrings, weren't worth five coppers, this was a very desperate statement to make.

A tiny smile came and quickly left Miss Bell's face. "Charlie, I know this must be difficult for you to understand, but the price of the gifts has nothing to do with it. Oh dear!" Miss Bell clasped her hands tightly beside a large pile of still-uncorrected class papers on her desk, stared at them for a moment, then sighed and looked at Charlotte. "I didn't want to tell you all the story, Charlie, because I didn't want to hurt or confuse you, but"— she sighed again—"I suppose I must. You remember, don't you, that I requested and received Mr. Chung's permission for you two girls to meet at recess?"

Charlotte nodded.

"What I didn't tell you was that he allowed it be-

166

cause I, as Anna's teacher, recommended it, but it was only on a trial basis. I really didn't see any reason to tell you that. In any event, now Mr. Chung feels that because of—of the *kind* of gifts you gave one another, *not* the cost of them, you aren't suitable friends for each other."

Miss Bell unclasped her hands, sat back in her chair, and looked as if she hoped that was the end of the explanation. But Charlotte must have looked blank. She felt blank. What was wrong with the kind of gifts they'd exchanged? She had loved the earrings. Anna had loved the scrapbook. If it wasn't how much they cost, what else was there to be wrong?

Miss Bell clasped her hands on her desk again. "You gave Anna a scrapbook of movie stars' pictures, didn't you?"

Charlotte nodded again.

"Well, as you probably know, Charlie, Anna isn't allowed to go to the movies. And it seems that Mr. Chung feels *anything* to do with movies is very frivolous and somehow—evil. So it looks as if he thinks anyone who would give his daughter a present that tells about movie stars is going to be a—well, a wicked influence, I suppose."

Miss Bell smiled grimly at the idea that the girl sitting in front of her, with tear-stained cheeks, scarred knees sticking out from a plaid skirt with two inches of let-down hem on it, and a grubby wet handkerchief in her hands, might be considered a wicked influence.

"And," she continued finally, "it also looks as if he feels that someone who would give a scrapbook as a gift must be a very young girl who possibly not only couldn't wear the earrings, but wouldn't appreciate anything so beautiful as carved jade."

"But I do love them, even if I can't wear them," Charlotte burst out. "I think they're beautiful!"

"I'm sure you do," said Miss Bell. "But Mr. Chung doesn't believe that. What it comes down to is that he feels your gift was wasted on Anna, and her gift was wasted on you, and that therefore your friendship is wasted on each other. I don't agree with that, but there doesn't seem to be anything I can do about it."

"Miss Bell, can't you talk to him and tell him? Oh, please!"

"I don't think it would do any good, Charlie. Oh!" Miss Bell had glanced up at the big clock on the wall over the blackboard. "I'm due at our teachers' meeting in ten minutes and haven't even begun on these papers yet. Charlie, I'm afraid you'll have to excuse me now."

"Miss Bell, please!" Charlotte had never been a pest with any grown-up except her own parents before. But she was sure Miss Bell understood the importance of the situation, that she had to exact a promise from her teacher to talk or write to Mr. Chung. She simply had to!

Miss Bell ran a weary hand through her hair so the hump on one side rose up even higher. "All right, I'll try to think of something. I can't promise anything, but I'll try."

"Oh, plea—" Charlotte began again.

"Charlie, I *said* I'd try, but I must get on with my work now!" There was a sharp note in Miss Bell's voice that hadn't been there before.

Charlotte rose slowly from the chair and walked to

the empty fifth grade desk where she'd laid her books. Her feet scuffed dejectedly on the floor.

"I'm sorry, Charlie," Miss Bell said. "I *will* try. We'll talk about it another time." Her voice trailed off as she studied the top paper from the pile on her desk. It was easy to see that her mind was already filled with un-corrected papers and teachers' meetings, and that Char-lotte Barrett had been dismissed not just from the room, but from her thoughts as well.

Crushed and miserable, Charlotte dragged home. This was the first time she had ever been spoken to sharply by Miss Bell, by any teacher. Things like that happened to people like Eddy Schmidt, who sat around in class chewing wads of paper to build up a supply of spitballs for recess, who never raised their hands with answers to questions because they never had the an-swers, and who kept desks that looked like pigpens.

Charlotte had felt that because of what had hap-pened with Anna, she and Miss Bell had a special re-lationship. Now that had ended. Suddenly Charlotte thought of the old, nearly-forgotten name she and Christene had once applied to Miss Bell—Miss Dumpy-mouse. That was exactly the right word for her. If she was still Cousin Philip's friend, and Mrs. Barrett *had* mentioned seeing them together, then Cousin Philip ought to be warned against her. Miss Bell had no right to speak to her sharply, thought Charlotte. Her eyes began to sting again, and her nose to run. She wiped them both angrily on her coat sleeve. She would not use the handkerchief Miss Bell had given her that was still in her pocket.

Half a block past the creek, Charlotte's dragging

footsteps quickened, and she began to walk faster and faster, almost running finally, away from school and Miss Bell toward home. Home! Where she could report the terrible things that had happened to her at school. Home! Where she would hear all the kind and sympathetic things she wanted to hear. Home! That was where Charlotte wanted most to be right then.

Deep in her own thoughts, she hardly noticed the strange fact that her father's car was parked at the front door of their house. She began to wonder about it only after she had rung the doorbell, then had rung it and rung it again, with nobody coming to let her in. She was about to run around to the back when the front door was cautiously opened a few inches, and Dossafoo's anxious face peered out. Behind Dossafoo, staring stiffly over his shoulder, was Coolie. When Dossafoo saw that it was Charlotte who'd been ringing the bell, he threw open the door.

Neither Dossafoo nor Coolie looked prepared to come to the front door. Coolie was covered with coal dust, and Dossafoo's work apron was smeared with chocolate cake batter and bristling with chicken feathers from the chicken he'd been plucking for dinner. Something was terribly wrong that it should be Dossafoo and Coolie dressed like that at the door instead of Liu opening it smoothly in his spotless white cotton gown.

"What's happened?" Charlotte cried. "Where's Liu? Where's Mother?"

Dossafoo rubbed the front of his apron nervously. "Very sick, Missy Charlie! Very sick!"

"Who's very sick?" Her first thought was that it must be her father.

"Young master," Dossafoo said. "Master Jamey."

Coolie bobbed his head up and down, up and down, like a Japanese kokeshi doll. His coal-blackened face looked stricken. Coolie and Jamey were very good friends. Just as Charlotte spent a lot of time bothering Dossafoo in the kitchen, Jamey followed Coolie around because the things Coolie did were often of the greatest interest to a small boy. Jamey loved to help Coolie pile coal into the furnace, bring it up to the fireplace in the den, or scrape paint off the drainpipes. And almost every time Mr. and Mrs. Barrett went out to dinner, Jamey went down to the servants' quarters, brought Coolie upstairs, pulled a chair up to the Victrola, which he wasn't supposed even to *touch*, wound it up, and put on his and Coolie's favorite record. Then he would climb down, and he and Coolie would stand reverently listening to "No Matter How Young the Prune May Be, He's Always Full of Wrinkles." The whole process would be repeated for the other side of the record— "Hey Diddle Diddle, the Cat and the Fiddle." After that, Coolie went back down to the basement. Both Charlotte and Christene knew this was going on, but they had never mentioned it to their mother or father.

"Jamey?" Charlotte asked.

Coolie's head bobbed up and down even faster. He looked as if he were going to cry.

Now Charlotte remembered Jamey's complaint that morning. Somehow he had managed to get himself brought home again, and had the whole household in an uproar about it. Desperate to report her grief to her mother, Charlotte was annoyed to think her problems would have to wait.

There seemed to be no further point in looking at

Dossafoo and Coolie's woebegone faces, so Charlotte started toward the stairs. Once she had determined that they were magnifying the situation out of all proportion, and that there was nothing seriously wrong with Jamey, she would drag her mother off somewhere to pour out her own misery.

But before Charlotte got past the second step, she heard voices and shuffling footsteps on the second floor and, looking up, saw her father coming down the stairs with a blanket-wrapped bundle in his arms. Behind him was her mother, followed by Liu carrying two suitcases, and then Amah Cho Mei, with Dusty at her heels.

"Watch out, sweetheart; we're coming through!" her father said.

"What's wrong? What happened?" Charlotte asked, staring at her father, but not moving away.

"Please, Charlie, step aside, won't you?" her father said. His voice wasn't angry, but it was taut, abrupt, and businesslike.

Crushed because she had come home looking for sympathy and understanding, only to be told tersely to "step aside," and because now suddenly she knew that something frightening *was* happening, only no one would tell her exactly what, Charlotte moved backwards down the two steps and pushed herself tightly against the wall.

Her father, with the cocoon of blankets in his arms, brushed past her. But her mother stepped close to Charlotte, allowing Liu and Amah Cho Mei to pass by and on out the door with Mr. Barrett. Her face appeared drawn, and there were tiny worry lines between her eyes.

172

"Charlie, Jamey has scarlet fever and has to go to the hospital. I had it years ago, so Dr. Bordwell says I'll be able to stay with him. Daddy will be back as soon as he's taken us to the hospital. Explain to Chrissy, will you, dear, when she gets home? Be good girls, now, and mind Daddy while I'm away. Don't be frightened. Everything is going to be fine."

Mrs. Barrett patted Charlotte on the cheek and tried to manage a reassuring smile. But all the smile told Charlotte was that everything might not be fine at all.

Scarlet fever! What was that? Charlotte had never heard of it before, but it must be serious if you had to go to the hospital with it. Scarlet fever! It sounded like something red and horrible. Was it worse than small-pox? Worse than *cholera?* Charlotte shivered.

Too numb to move, she stared at the gaping front door where moments before the small parade had passed, carrying Jamey to the hospital with scarlet fever. How, Charlotte wondered, did you get this scarlet fever? Like cholera, could you catch it from—eating something? Something like a piece of sesame candy from a shop in Chinese City?

Charlotte had never told her parents about the sesame candy Jamey had eaten. She had come very close to confessing it when her father had talked to her about the seriousness of what she had done, going alone with Jamey to Chinese City. But in the end she'd said nothing. Her crime seemed terrible enough without reporting that part of it. And luckily, Jamey, in the excitement of that day, had somehow forgotten to tell anyone about the candy himself.

Supposing it turned out that scarlet fever was something that could be prevented with shots if you only knew about it in time? Would she have the courage to confess about the sesame candy then?

Charlotte wished that she could have seen Jamey inside the blankets before he left. Not seeing him made it all the more mysterious, more terrifying. Did you—could you *die* from scarlet fever? If only *she* had eaten the candy instead of Jamey!

Then a monstrous thought leaped into her head. No, it couldn't have just leaped into her head. It must have been there all along—that she was glad she hadn't eaten the candy, that it was Jamey going to the hospital instead of herself. It wasn't that she wanted Jamey to have scarlet fever; it was just that she didn't want to have it herself, to have to go to the hospital, perhaps even to die!

But how could she be thinking that? How could an ordinary eleven-year-old girl have such hideous thoughts? What kind of person was this Charlotte Barrett?

Charlotte heard the motor start up outside the house. When the sounds of the car had faded away, the servants came back into the house. Coolie was carrying Dusty, who was whining softly, and Amah was wringing her hands and moaning, "Ai ya! Ai ya!" Charlotte felt she couldn't bear to see them, to see anyone. Turning away quickly, she ran up the stairs to her room, slammed the door, and threw herself face down on the bed, as if by blacking out her eyes, she could black out her mind as well.

What kind of person am I? Charlotte asked herself over and over. A hopeless, impossible person. No wonder Christene had kicked her out of their room. Christene was right—she was a pest and a baby. And her mother and father were right, too—she was thoughtless, careless, and impulsive, and she had no sense of responsibility. Now she was a liar, too, because wasn't *not* mentioning the sesame candy a lie? And hadn't she lied to Anna about Beverly Showberg, trying to impress her with knowing a real live movie star, then going on to make that stupid scrapbook? Mr. Chung was right in considering Charlotte an unsuitable friend for Anna. She *was* an unsuitable friend, and an unsuitable younger sister, and now an unsuitable older sister as well!

How did you go about being suitable? Why wasn't she able to grow up in a nice, neat, uncomplicated, suitable way like Christene, for instance? Christene, who had found a friend without even trying, who was busy going to parties, and who had nothing to worry about but what style to wear her hair. Christene, whose biggest tragedy had been not getting Cousin Philip to pay any attention to her friend Moira.

Why, Charlotte wondered, couldn't she, like Christene, be suddenly grown-up, without having to go through the tortures of getting there? Could it be because she didn't really want to grow up, to give up the way she had always felt about Christmas, about her Huntley & Palmer treasure box, about peering through stair railings at cocktail parties and making up stories for Jamey, about watching the hot noodle man and having talks with Dossafoo in the kitchen? Could it be because she was afraid to grow up? Afraid to give up the Charlotte she had always known for a Charlotte she didn't know at all?

Pest! Baby! Unsuitable! Liar, liar, liar!

Charlotte clenched her hands into fists and beat on the bed beside her pillow.

"Stink!" It was a word she hadn't said in so long she had almost forgotten it.

But it was only a word. It, and a hundred words like it, if she said them over a million times, could never change anything. Charlotte opened her eyes and, her face still on the pillow, saw her family of Chinese dolls smiling at her impassively from across the room. They were old friends, but today they offered no comfort. For a long time, she lay staring at them, and then, finally, the tears began rolling down her cheeks and onto her pillow. Because as much as she didn't want to have scarlet fever, Charlotte didn't want Jamey to have it either. She loved her little brother and didn't want him to die.

FOURTEEN

SOMEHOW school ended. Somehow the lilacs and forsythia in the garden, the acacia trees that lined their street, had bloomed and faded. Now, somehow, it was summer. And we are on our way to Peitaho again, thought Charlotte, as if no time had passed between, as if nothing had ever happened.

Her legs curled up under her, she stared through the window of their compartment in the train carrying them to the seashore. Her mind was lulled by the sight of field after flat green field of gao liang rolling by; the farmers, in their faded blue jackets and pagoda-shaped straw hats, standing still as statues with their oxen as they stared back at the train; the tall mounds of grass-covered earth that were graves; willow trees hanging motionless over lily ponds; and clay-walled villages that looked like toys spilled against the foot of a faraway hill. It seemed as if the summer afternoon had fallen asleep in the hot sun and could not be awakened, even by clucking chickens in a village train station or by the small children who swarmed around the train with hands outstretched for coppers, not at all concerned that fully-clothed foreign children stared curiously out the train windows at their sunbaked naked bodies.

The soothing clickety-clack of the train wheels on the track seemed to be marking the villages, the fields, the miles, that lay between Charlotte and the big brick house on the corner that was home, the school by the river, the dusty playground, making everything that had happened in those places seem unreal, as if she had only read about them in a book.

But the sight of Jamey sitting across from her, his face still so thin and wan that his dark eyes seemed twice their size, of Christene carefully turning the pages of her book with polished fingernails, or her own cotton skirt with the bright unfaded band of color at the bottom showing clearly where it had been let down, all cried out that this wasn't the summer of the year before, that time *had* passed, that all the unreal things *had* happened.

Moira Evans had happened. The puppies Dusty and Maximilian had happened. The terrifying adventure in Chinese City, Jamey's scarlet fever, and Number-three Yueh daughter's wedding had all happened. And Anna had happened.

It was difficult to remember that Anna had ever been more than just a classroom acquaintance. All Charlotte could see in her mind now was the picture of Anna, with her brother William, scurrying into the classroom in the morning, huddled over her books at recess in some out-of-the-way corner of the playground, being the same frightened, lonely rabbit she'd been at the beginning. Sometimes their eyes would meet in class, saying something their stilted conversations about schoolwork could never say, but that made it even more difficult for Charlotte to accept the fact that they had become strangers again. She would never speak to Anna again about what had happened. She would not force Anna to talk about it. To do that was to be a pest. She had learned what it meant to be a pest, and she would not be one with Anna.

As for the earrings, they began to look strange and out of place in the Huntley & Palmer treasure box, so Charlotte finally gave them to her mother to keep.

"Perhaps," her mother said, "next Christmas you might ask for a Peking jewelry box like Chris's, and then you can take them back to keep in it."

"Perhaps," said Charlotte.

Beyond that, school was school. Still smarting from their after-school conversation, Charlotte had determined that she would be cool and distant with Miss Bell, never raise her hand in class or offer to clean the blackboard. But the first time Miss Bell had smiled at her—it was actually the moment she walked into class the next day—Charlotte had smiled right back, and that was the end of that. To be Charlotte was *not* to be cool and distant. She had never been that with anyone in her life.

One good thing that came out of the Chinese City adventure and that made the loss of Charlotte's recesses with Anna at least bearable was becoming better friends with Skinny Buttrick and Barry Dameron, especially Barry. Before the end of school, Eddy Schmidt had a birthday party. It was his fourteenth or fifteenth —Charlotte couldn't remember which—and all the sixth grade, except for Anna and William who had been invited but didn't come, and most of the seventh grade, those who had been Eddy's classmates during the first of his two years in fifth grade, were there. The girls, including Charlotte, had all squealed with horror when somebody suggested playing "post office," but they'd played it anyway, and Barry kept asking for Charlotte. He was teased about it, but went right on doing it. Though Charlotte wouldn't have admitted it to anyone in the world, she liked being called out of the room by Barry. She liked all of it, even the teasing.

But in the end, nothing made up entirely for losing Anna. Charlotte's father had been right. You might replace something lost with something else, but it would never be the same as the thing that was gone.

The train shattered the afternoon with a piercing whistle as it slowed down to pass through a village. A pack of wonk dogs rushed at the train, barking wildly, but stopped short of it finally when they could see that, for all their noise, the train was going right on. One of the dogs was black and looked like Maximilian. Not the puppy Maximilian, but the grown-up one.

Charlotte had been taken to see him at Aunty Mabel's house just before they'd left Tientsin. Only now there was no more puppy Maximilian. The dog Charlotte saw was simply a big black wonk with a skinny tail, small beady eyes, and a large red mouth. And it was difficult to remember that Aunty Mabel had taken him only "as a favor to Charlotte," for she had him sleeping in a satin-lined basket and wearing a jeweled collar, and she held him on her lap the whole time they were visiting. Although Charlotte was pleased to be relieved of the duty, she thought a big black dog dangling off Aunty Mabel's lap looked even more ridiculous than *she* had. It was almost too ridiculous to laugh at. It made her uncomfortable listening to Aunty Mabel talk baby talk to Maximilian, and she was glad when they went home. Maximilian was Aunty Mabel's dog now. He had become a stranger.

Stranger! Did everyone become a stranger finally, like Anna, and like Christene? Christene had been one for months, and was still one. Even though Moira Evans had left for America with her family, Christene hadn't changed toward Charlotte, or anyone. Most of the time she closed herself in her room or played records or read. In September she would go away to high school near Peking. And then, thought Charlotte, she will become more of a stranger than ever.

Even Jamey had been a stranger for a while, when he had been brought home from the hospital. He and Charlotte had looked at one another with shy eyes and had had to become acquainted all over again. But for them, it hadn't taken long. Soon Charlotte was busy making up stories to tell him, rushing up to his room the moment she returned from school. Jamey had developed what Charlotte breathlessly informed Barry and Skinny were "complications," so he never did get back to kindergarten. This meant Charlotte had to think up lots of things to entertain him because, as she told herself, her mother and father and Amah and Coolie certainly couldn't do it all.

One of the things she did was to ask Coolie to wrap Jamey in blankets and carry him to a rocking chair by the window, where Jamey could see Number-three Yueh daughter's wedding procession. There Charlotte, because of her recess "lessons" with Anna, could explain all that had gone before it, all the things that happened, that had *always* happened when the daughter and son of two Chinese families were married according to ancient customs.

"Jamey, when we're in Peitaho next summer—" Charlotte began thoughtfully after the wedding procession had passed, and they were staring out at the almost-deserted street.

"Are we going to Peitaho?" Jamey asked.

"Yes!"

"Even if there are bandits?" Jamey's eyes widened. He wasn't making up the idea. There could be bandits. Jamey had heard from Charlotte herself how in the summer whole bands of them could disappear like magic into the great fields of gao liang, the corn that grew ten feet tall, to reappear *anywhere* along the roads and railroad tracks. Charlotte had even made up a story for Jamey about a Bandit Ling, who had ugly long black mustaches and fierce black eyes, and whose sole aim in life was to blow up the main bridge between Tientsin and Peitaho.

"We went last year and there were bandits, weren't there?" said Charlotte.

"Yes."

"Well then!"

Jamey said nothing more about it. He was like Charlotte. If something happened once, there was no reason for it not to happen again and again. It was all the explanation he needed.

"Anyway," said Charlotte, "when we're in Peitaho this summer, Daddy will come up to spend his vacation with us the way he did last year, only this year he might bring Cousin Philip with him, so I think we should have an entertainment."

"Why?" asked Jamey.

"I don't know. I just think we should. So I'm going to put on a play. Well, not a real play, just a—a kind of performance. And, Jamey, you can do it with me!"

"I don't think I want to."

"Why not?"

"Because I don't know what it is."

"Oh," said Charlotte. "Well, what this performance is going to be is a Chinese wedding. Not a real one, just a pretend one. I'll be the bride, and you can be the groom, and we'll get Amah and Dossafoo to be—oh, I don't know what yet, but they'll be something in it."

Jamey looked puzzled. "Why can't Coolie be in it?"

"Oh, Jamey!" Charlotte gave an exasperated sigh. "I just forgot to *say* Coolie. He can be in it."

Jamey carefully rolled up the corner of his blanket, thinking this over. After a few moments, the corners of his mouth turned up in a small, secret smile. "Then I can be in it, too."

"Good!" Charlotte leaped up from the arm of the rocker, hugged herself, and whirled around. "Oh! Oh! Oh! Jamey, it's going to be such fun, fun, fun!"

"Charlie?"

"What?"

"How about Chrissy? Won't she be in it, too?"

Charlotte stopped whirling. "No, I don't think so," she said abruptly. "She'll probably be—be busy. We'll do it ourselves, Jamey."

Yes, of course Christene would be busy. She was "too busy" for everything these days.

Charlotte glanced now at Christene, reading as

usual, and at Jamey and Mrs. Barrett, who were both napping. Then she turned back to the window, trying to amuse herself finally by breathing little patches of steam on the glass and watching them slowly melt away. She was getting tired of this, too, when suddenly the train whistle pierced the sleepy afternoon.

"Mother, Jamey, everyone! We're coming to the bridge!" Charlotte cried.

It was impossible not to rush to look out when they crossed the main bridge between Peitaho and Tientsin that ran over an unbelievably long, deep ravine. Besides the terror of the bridge itself, there was something else to worry about. Charlotte may have made up Bandit Ling, but it was absolutely true that the bridge had been blown up time and time again by soldiers in some local war or by bandits. Mrs. Barrett, Jamey, and even Christene stood around Charlotte, frozen with a kind of horrible fascination as the train slowed to a crawl, and then began, almost painfully, to inch out onto the bridge.

"Do you think we'll see any bandits?" Jamey whispered. It wasn't surprising that he should whisper. You had the feeling when crossing the bridge that even the sound of voices was enough to hurl the train off the tracks into the ravine.

"I hope not," Charlotte whispered back.

"Well, I hope we do!"

"Jamey!"

"Well, I do. Charlie, should we start now?"

"Yes," said Charlotte, "now!" And she drew in a deep breath.

The year before, Charlotte and Christene had decided that it was a good idea to hold your breath as the train went across the bridge. Of course, you couldn't possibly hold just one breath, but you tried to take as few breaths as possible, holding each one as long as you could. It seemed to afford some kind of magical protection. Deep down inside, you knew it didn't really, but even deeper down inside than that, you knew it did. Charlotte had instructed Jamey in this before they left home, and he was prepared to hold his breath until he burst.

But Charlotte said nothing about it to Christene. Why bother? Christene would consider it silly this year.

The train moved out onto the bridge, inch by tortured inch, and then, when it was halfway across, stopped with a terrible shudder, hanging poised over nothing for at least thirty horrifying seconds. Charlotte, her chest aching from holding her breath, turned her head stiffly to see what the others were doing. Was she only imagining it? Or was Christene holding her breath, too? Charlotte turned back quickly so Christene wouldn't catch her staring, and took another deep breath of air.

Then, at last, they were on the other side, and they were safe. As everyone else drew a sigh of relief, Jamey threw himself back on the padded seat, happily exhausted with his efforts.

"Well, that's that," said Mrs. Barrett.

"We saved ourselves," said Jamey.

"Yes, we did. Chrissy?" Charlotte hesitated.

"What?" Christene had returned to her seat and picked up her book.

"Were you holding your breath, too?"

Christene shrugged. "I don't know."

"Well, *were* you?"

"Charlie, what difference does it make?" Christene said, and quickly turned her eyes down to her book again, closing the conversation.

But suddenly it did make a difference.

The house they would have in Peitaho, the same one they'd stayed in the year before, had only three bedrooms. Christene and Charlotte would share a room, as they had the previous summer. They would be roommates again. So, yes, quite suddenly, though Charlotte would never have been able to explain why, it seemed to make a great deal of difference whether Christene, along with Charlotte, had held her breath as they crossed the bridge.

FIFTEEN

PEITAHO, the Chinese summer-resort village that lay along the seacoast like a long string of beads, seemed the same, all beautifully the same as it had been the year before. The same sunbaked dirt roads lined with small gray cottages and pink-blossomed mimosa trees, the same sleepy sounds of cicadas grinding, and the same rich, hot smells of dust and donkeys. It was all there to greet them as they stepped off the train, as if everything had been hanging suspended since the end of last summer, like Sleeping Beauty's kingdom, waiting for them to return. Here, nothing had changed. Really nothing! thought Charlotte wonderingly.

Small and gray and shaggy, one looking not much different from the other, the donkeys clustered around the station, patiently swishing flies off their backs with their tails, as each master good-naturedly called out his donkey's special qualities to young missy or young master clambering down from the train.

Then Charlotte laughed, because her mother said the very same thing she'd said the year before. "Of course you can't have a donkey ride now, Jamey. We'll all take rickshaws and see about donkey rides later." And that rickshaw ride probably would be the last the children would take that summer. Their mother might ride in them, since there were no cars traveling the roads that threaded the village to the seacoast, but the children always rode donkeys. Always, said Charlotte firmly to herself.

Nor had their house changed. Even though Charlotte knew that the house had been boarded up and locked for the winter, she found it hard to believe that this spreading summer cottage hadn't been sitting there exactly the way they'd left it the year before, with the same snapdragons and delphiniums and daisies in bloom in the garden, and the same wicker chairs, with the faded rose cretonne cushions, scattered across the veranda, looking serenely out over the cliffs toward the sea.

And once they were settled, the calm, peaceful vacation days began, one following the other, in the same full, familiar pattern of the summer before.

In the morning they went to the beach, sometimes finding it so deserted it seemed like their very own. They swam in water often as clear and smooth as a melted blue glass marble, with the sand under their feet like velvet ripples. They could jump off a Chinese junk, stationed in the water just for the pleasure of swimmers. Or, if they didn't feel like swimming, they could hunt for pink-and-purple-lined shells, as beautiful as a sunset.

Returning from the beach, they took baths in a

strange tin tub right in their bedroom. Coolie had to fill the tub with water stored in the courtyard and heated on the kitchen stove. It took buckets and buckets to produce even five or six inches of water in the bottom of the tub, so Charlotte, as the younger, often had to take her bath in Christene's soapy, sandy, used bath water. It was no longer even lukewarm. At home in Tientsin, she would have complained bitterly, but here, because it was Peitaho, she accepted the insult without a murmur.

After tiffin, the midday meal, they took naps as they'd always done, as everyone did, in Peitaho, falling asleep to the drowsy sound of scissor grinders, their name for cicadas, or a faraway donkey braying in the hot sun. Then, in the afternoon, they took long walks, or sat on the veranda watching a traveling Chinese merchant unpack his faded blue cloth bundle and pull out a stream of treasures—embroidered linens, flowered porcelain bowls, carved rose quartz figurines, turquoise and jade jewelry. Or they curled up on the cushions of a huge wicker chair, munched endless bars of Nestle's chocolate, and read and read and read. In the evening, though it was difficult because there were no electric lights, they went on reading, only half hearing the moths thumping against the glass chimneys of their gas lamps.

In Peitaho, Charlotte could almost forget that anything bad had happened to her, and almost wonder if anything bad could ever happen again.

Mr. Barrett wrote of the cholera epidemic in Tientsin, but it was only words on paper to Charlotte. Mrs. Barrett read the letter to Christene and Charlotte on the sunny veranda one morning. Though her face was drawn, she read in a calm, steady voice and even managed a laugh when Mr. Barrett wrote, "Philip has moved in with me. I knew you'd agree that he should. Charlie will be amused to know that he and Dusty are sharing her bed in the playroom. Liu is taking excellent care of both of us. He has us on a diet consisting solely of what he terms 'vellee safe' over-boiled chicken, melba toast, and scotch and sodas. I can tell you that Philip and I are already thoroughly sick of the chicken and toast."

Charlotte did laugh at Cousin Philip choosing the playroom, pleased that it was now her room, and promptly dismissed the cholera epidemic from her mind. It had no reality, anyway. After the letter had been read, she and Christene and Amah Cho Mei and Jamey went to the beach. She and Jamey built the best sand castle they'd made that summer.

Four days later there was a second letter. That one wasn't read to them because it came to Amah Cho Mei. Mrs. Barrett only told Christene and Charlotte that evening before dinner that Amah's married daughter had died of cholera. Charlotte wondered guiltily why she couldn't feel anything about it, then decided that perhaps she wasn't expected to. Although Mrs. Barrett told Amah she didn't have to do it, Amah still came in as usual to take Jamey to bed. Her oiled black hair drawn back neatly into a bun, her white jacket spotless and unmussed, she looked comfortingly ordinary to Charlotte. After dinner, Charlotte and Christene played Fish under the gas lamp on the veranda. Night beetles clicked against the glass shade. The cool air was sweet with roses. Charlotte and Christene each ate a whole bar of Nestle's chocolate with filberts. The death had no reality at all.

Then, in the deep deadness of night, ghastly, frightening sounds poured into Charlotte's dream and woke her. At first, her mind still heavy with sleep, she lay thinking that this was a part of her dream. Then she stiffened as the terrible moaning, wailing, sobbing sounds continued to fill the courtyard and press into the room. They were not like anything she had ever heard before. They didn't even seem human. But Charlotte knew, without being told, that they came from Amah, giving over her grief for her lost child to the night.

It was finally real. It couldn't be blocked out with Fish or chocolate bars or sand castles at the beach. Trembling, Charlotte threw her sheet over her head and pushed her fingers into her ears.

She lay that way for what seemed like hours, stiff and cold with a nameless mixture of pity and terror. And then a circle of soft light shone through her sheet.

"Shhhhh. Charlie, it's me, Chrissy."

Charlotte slowly peered over her sheet and saw Christene standing by her bed, a flashlight in her hand. For a moment, the girls only looked at one another, owl-eyed from having listened too long, sleepless, to the sounds of their Amah's grief.

"What is it, Chrissy?" Charlotte wondered why she felt it necessary to whisper.

"I just discovered something I thought you'd want to see," Christene whispered back. "Here, hold the flashlight while I light the lamp." She thrust the flashlight into Charlotte's hand, then lit a match, lifted the glass

chimney of the lamp on her dresser, and held the flame
to the wick. Quickly she turned down the wick so it
gave off the least possible amount of light.

"All right, you can turn off the flash now," Christene
said.

When Charlotte did, there was only a small, eerie
glow around the dresser.

"Come on, Charlie! Come see!" Christene said.

Charlotte laid the flashlight on the bed table,
dropped her feet onto the cold floor, and padded barefoot to where Christene stood by the dresser. Christene
picked up the lamp and lowered it toward the bottom
drawer, the one that held their emergency sweaters and
warm clothes, and was rarely opened. It was open now.

"Look! Look inside!" Christene commanded.

Charlotte lowered her nose into the drawer. "I don't
see anything."

"There! In there!" Christene pointed to a back
corner.

192

"Oh, Chrissy," breathed Charlotte. "When did you find them?"

"Just before I called you. I barely heard the scratching noises, but I came to investigate anyway. It must have been the mother. Charlie, I think she must have just finished having them. I think they've just been born. I opened the drawer yesterday looking for my blue jersey, and there wasn't even a nest then."

As Christene finished saying this, she and Charlotte looked suddenly at one another, listening. All at once, from the courtyard, there was only silence. A cricket chirped hesitantly in the garden.

"She's stopped," Christene said flatly.

"Oh, Chrissy!" said Charlotte.

Their eyes held for a moment, and then slowly turned and looked down again into the drawer at the nest of newborn mice.

"Will she start again?" Charlotte asked.

"No, I don't believe she will," Christene said. "I believe it has ended, Charlie."

Charlotte put her hands over her sunbrowned arms and shivered. They went on staring into the drawer. Then, after a while, the cricket finished his song.

"Chrissy, they look just like pink jelly beans," Charlotte said.

"With tails," said Christene.

"Yes, with tails," Charlotte echoed solemnly, as if it were the most important piece of information in the world.

"How many do you count?" Christene asked.

"Seven," said Charlotte.

"I count six—no, you're right. There are seven." Christene lowered her head toward the drawer and then said softly, "What do you think we ought to do about them?"

Charlotte hesitated. The question had startled her because they were Christene's mice, not hers.

"I mean," Christene added hurriedly, "do you think we ought to—tell anyone?"

Charlotte knew what Christene meant. Years ago, when they were very small, they had trustingly reported the discovery of baby mice to their mother and father, and the mice had been drowned.

"What do *you* think?" asked Charlotte.

"I asked *you*," Christene replied. "Do you think we should tell anyone?"

Not to tell about the mice was a lie. Charlotte had suffered from a lie already. Even though she'd found out later that Jamey's scarlet fever had come from a little boy at Alfred Wang's birthday party and not from the sesame candy from Chinese City, she had still suffered from the lie for a long time. But for some strange reason, Christene was forcing her to make the decision about the mice, and she knew that whatever she decided, they would do.

"No," said Charlotte.

"You're sure?" Christene asked.

"Yes."

"It's decided then." Christene slid the drawer shut gently but firmly. "We'll watch over them and feed them. And we won't tell anyone about it. Come on, we'd better get back to our beds. The mother mouse must be frantic by now."

She set the lamp on the dresser. Reaching to turn down the wick, she turned suddenly instead to Charlotte. "You don't have to worry, Charlie. It will be all

194

right." She put her hand out and hesitantly touched a puffed sleeve of Charlotte's faded yellow pajamas, ones that used to be hers. "I promise you it will be all right."

Then she quickly put out the light and ran to her bed.

That night changed Charlotte's whole summer, at least where Christene was concerned. They'd been getting along well enough in their room together. The atmosphere was polite, at least, and with Charlotte trying her best not to be a pest in any way, they weren't having squabbles. Without Moira Evans around, they went everywhere and did everything together. But there was a difference from the summer before, and the difference was in Christene. She had grown up since then.

Now, with the discovery of the mice, Christene suddenly became fun again, the Christene of last summer instead of this one. When they went to the beach, she balanced with Charlotte on the low stone walls, instead of walking sedately on the road. She spent far less time basting herself with coconut butter and worrying about getting an even tan, and spent more of it having swimming races with Charlotte to the junk, building sand castles, and hunting shells. Charlotte even noticed, but carefully didn't mention it, that Christene was letting the polish on her nails get scraggly and not bothering to take it off and replace it.

Charlotte wished that the magic of the baby mice could remain forever, but the day came, as it had to, when they looked in the drawer and found the nest empty, the mice gone. Gone with them were the secret trips to the bedroom with food from the dining table hidden in Charlotte or Christene's pockets, gone the last looks into the drawer before they went to bed at night, and gone the secret, mysterious references to "it" and "them."

But if the mice were gone, there was now something else to look forward to. Mr. Barrett and Cousin Philip were to arrive in only two weeks, and Charlotte had to begin preparations for the wedding performance.

"Be in it with us!" she asked Christene one day.

"I wouldn't mind so much," Christene said, "if *she* weren't going to be here."

"I don't know what difference it makes," Charlotte replied.

"Well, it does," said Christene.

She was Miss Bell. Mrs. Barrett had learned through a letter from Cousin Philip that Miss Bell was in Peitaho visiting friends. He had mentioned that he would be seeing her, so Mrs. Barrett had sent a note inviting her for dinner and the little entertainment Charlotte had planned.

Charlotte was thrilled, but Christene had remained cool about the idea. Now, because of Miss Bell, she was refusing to be in the wedding performance.

"I'm sorry, Charlie. I really don't want to be in it. I'll help you rehearse it if you want, though." It was all she would agree to. This wasn't what Charlotte wanted, but she was happy to have Christene doing anything at all about the entertainment.

Then there was the problem of Amah Cho Mei.

"Should I ask her to be in the play?" Charlotte asked her mother.

"Of course you should," Mrs. Barrett replied firmly.

"You're asking Dossafoo and Coolie, aren't you? Amah would be hurt if you didn't include her."

Charlotte hesitated. "That's not—that's not what I meant."

"I know what you meant, Charlie," her mother said. "But I still think you should ask. If she's not—ready, she'll say so, I'm sure. You know, dear, it may not be something you think about, but Amah does love you three children." She looked closely at Charlotte. "Are you shy, Charlie? Would you like me to ask Amah?"

Charlotte shook her head slowly. "No, I'll do it."

Later, she reported back to her mother that Amah would be in the play. "She *wants* to be, Mother," Charlotte said happily.

"There, you see," her mother replied calmly, and then kissed her on the nose. Charlotte couldn't understand what the kiss was all about.

The two weeks flew by at a dizzying speed. There were so many things to do and so few hours to do them in.

There were the properties to collect—red and green paper, an apple, rice bowls and chopsticks, a scroll, a sesamum oil lamp, and even a goose. The list seemed endless.

The costumes, fortunately, could be simple. Amah Cho Mei, Dossafoo, and Coolie would wear their own clothes, while Charlotte, as the bride, and Jamey, the groom, would wear their mandarin beach coats, Charlotte's decorated with ribbons and flowers.

Finally, there were the rehearsals. Each evening, with a great air of mystery, Charlotte or Jamey ushered Mrs. Barrett to her room, where she had to remain for an hour or more while they rehearsed on the veranda. The rehearsals, Charlotte found, were the hardest work of all. She had never had anything to do with a play before, and she marveled at how something that had seemed quite simple at the beginning could end up so complicated—where Amah Cho Mei should sit or Dossafoo stand, whether the wedding procession should go all around the veranda or simply across it. And she had a terrible time with Coolie and Jamey, who kept grinning at each other and wouldn't be serious. But it was fun, and the hours and the days raced by.

Sharing the secret of the mouse family with Christene, then having her sister help with rehearsals, the wedding performance rehearsed and ready, and her father, Cousin Philip, and Miss Bell there to see it—Charlotte felt certain that nothing could add to the happiness of her summer. And then the letter came.

They were all coming home from the train together, Charlotte holding her father's hand, Jamey riding on Cousin Philip's shoulders, Mrs. Barrett and Christene walking alongside them. Charlotte was explaining how much better her nose looked this week than it had four weeks ago when it was red and peeling from sunburn, and Jamey was telling how he had collected a whole bucket of jellyfish stingers. Everyone was talking and laughing at once because this was Cousin Philip's first time in Peitaho, and he wanted to know all about it. And they were trying to tell him all about it *all* at the same time. Then, when they were almost home, Charlotte's father quietly slipped his hand into the pocket of his linen jacket and pulled out a white envelope.

"Here's something for you, Charlie."

"For me?" asked Charlotte.

198

"You are Charlotte Barrett, aren't you?"

Charlotte nodded.

"Then this *must* be for you," said Mr. Barrett, and he handed her the envelope.

" 'To Miss Charlotte Barrett,' " Charlotte read to herself. " 'No. 1, Newchwang Loo, Tientsin, China.' " Then she turned the envelope over and drew in a sharp breath.

Hardly realizing what she was doing after that, she choked out an "Excuse me, please!" and ran down the road to their house, across the veranda, through the living room, and into her bedroom. Shutting the door behind her, she dropped down onto her bed and sat there, staring at the envelope. She was still staring at it when Christene burst into the room a few minutes later.

"Charlie, Daddy said your letter was from Anna Chung! Charlie! Haven't you opened it yet?"

Charlotte shook her head.

"Why not?"

"I'm afraid to," Charlotte said.

"Don't be silly. You've got to open it sometime. You might just as well open it now."

Slowly, carefully, Charlotte peeled up the flap of the envelope, pulled out the letter, and read to herself:

Dear Charlie,

Because I do not know if you have left Tientsin for the summer, I am sending this letter to your home here. I hope very much that it will reach you soon.

The reason I am writing to you is to tell you something that has happened. It has made me very happy, and I hope it will make you happy, too.

Before the end of school, our teacher, Miss Bell,

gave me a book to read and to keep. It is a book of many stories, and one of them has the name "The Gift of the Magi," written by Mr. O. Henry. In this story, a young man sells his gold watch to buy for his young wife a set of combs for her long and beautiful hair, while she at the same time has sold her hair to buy a chain for his watch. At the end of his story, Mr. Henry says, "But in a last word to the wise of these days let it be said that of all who give gifts these two were the wisest. Of all who give and receive gifts, such as they are the wisest. Everywhere they are the wisest. They are the magi."

Miss Bell said she hoped that I might ask our Chinese teacher to translate this story so that my father could read it. I did as Miss Bell asked, and my father read the story. I was afraid that the story made my father angry, because after he had finished it, he said nothing to me for many days.

Yesterday he spoke to me of the story. He said that at first it did make him angry, and that he was angry with Miss Bell that she should waste his time. Now he thinks that just as the people in the story are wise, so is Miss Bell wise. He believes now that what he has done is a mistake, and he wishes to ask the forgiveness of your family. I believe he will later speak to them himself. He has said that if they allow our friendship to continue, he hopes they will also allow you to honor us by coming to our home. I do not need to tell you that this is my hope also.

My father has not yet given me back the beautiful scrapbook you made for me, but I am (is this the correct thing that I say?) keeping my fingers crossed.

200

This morning my father said to my mother that he thinks perhaps Shirley Temple is not such an evil influence after all.

I hope you will answer my letter soon.

Your friend,
Anna Chung

When she had finished reading, Charlotte sat staring at the letter just as she'd stared at the envelope.

"Well, what did she say?"

Christene's voice seemed to burst in from nowhere. Charlotte had forgotten all about her sister standing there waiting. Numbly, she shook her head.

"Charlie! What did she say? Is it good or bad?"

Charlotte only shook her head again and held out the letter to Christene.

"Do you want me to read it myself?"

Charlotte nodded, so Christene took the letter.

Charlotte flopped backwards on the bed, and as Christene read the letter to herself, she lay staring at a slender cobweb on the ceiling that was waving in the breeze from their open window. And it wasn't until she felt the tears rolling down the sides of her face that she even knew she was crying.

SIXTEEN

ALTHOUGH all the lamps in the house and on the veranda had been turned down, there was still enough light at eight o'clock in the evening for Charlotte, peering nervously through the cracks of the makeshift curtain in front of the veranda stage, to see the audience assembled and ready for her play. Her mother and father were seated together on the wicker couch, while Cousin Philip, in white shirt, gray flannels, and tennis shoes, was perched on the veranda railing, one leg drawn up, leaning against a post, and looking, Charlotte thought, unbelievably handsome. Miss Bell and Christene were in the chairs to one side of him. And there were two more guests, too. At the last moment, Mrs. Barrett had decided to include in the evening Mr. and Mrs. Carney, the people Miss Bell was visiting. So it was a much larger audience than Charlotte had ever expected, gathered before the make-believe stage— much more talking—much more laughter. Suddenly she wished desperately that she was out there with all of them, instead of where she was.

The curtain she stood behind was only Dossafoo and Coolie standing on chairs and holding up a lienza, a matchstick bamboo shade. It had seemed all right when she'd planned it. Better than all right. The bamboo shade, along with everything else, had seemed quite wonderful when she was preparing for the performance. Now it all appeared homemade. Babyish! Charlotte couldn't understand why her feelings about it had changed so much in less than twenty-four hours. But somehow it seemed to stem from the arrival of Cousin Philip.

The three of them—Christene, Jamey, and Charlotte—had gone swimming with him that morning. Later, they had all gone for a donkey ride. Along the way, they had passed Charlotte's favorite Peitaho street vendor, the man who modeled figurines from rice paste, and Cousin Philip had insisted that they halt the donkey parade long enough to have a figurine modeled for each of them. It was fascinating to watch the modeling man at work, his nimble fingers fashioning in minutes the wonderfully intricate figures that he would end up putting on a bamboo stick and handing to a lucky buyer. Jamey chose his usual tiger; Charlotte, a fisherman complete with a straw cape, lantern, and fishing pole; and Christene, a beautiful Chinese actress with narrow whitened face, almond eyes, and ornate costume. Charlotte loved her fisherman, but when Cousin Philip mentioned laughingly that the actress was beautiful, but not so beautiful as its owner, Charlotte wished she'd chosen something more "beautiful" than a fisherman.

Actually, she was already disgruntled at Cousin Philip's behavior toward Christene. All day long he'd treated her as if she were a grown lady instead of just a girl not yet fourteen. He'd helped her up onto the junk when they were swimming (which, Charlotte thought disgustedly, Christene was perfectly able to manage by herself); offered a hand when she prepared to mount her donkey; stood by solicitously when she was ready to get off; asked her if she *wasn't* tired or *was* something else; and generally lumped Charlotte in with Jamey, letting her scramble around for herself. It wasn't surprising that Christene should arrive home from the donkey ride with her face flushed and eyes sparkling, after all this special treatment. Now Christene, who'd been smart enough to refuse to be in the wedding performance, was on the veranda, being very dignified and grown-up, laughing at Cousin Philip's jokes. There was something about it, Charlotte thought, that seemed terribly unjust.

Nonetheless, it was now eight o'clock. A performance had been promised, and a performance there would have to be. Charlotte tiptoed to her seat opposite Jamey, sat down, and nodded to Dossafoo and Coolie. At her signal, they rolled up the screen and ran with it into the living room, then quickly returned, Dossafoo to station himself beside Charlotte's chair, and Coolie beside Jamey's.

The seven-member audience applauded enthusiastically, and then Coolie and Jamey did exactly what Charlotte was afraid they'd do, grin at one another. Jamey ended by throwing his hands to his face, dissolved in giggles. It wasn't until Mrs. Barrett had spoken to him from the audience that he grew serious again. Her face burning with embarrassment, Charlotte rose from her chair, folded her hands under her chin, and bowed.

"Honorable guests, we welcome you to our performance of a Chinese wedding. I am Number-two Ling daughter, and Dossafoo plays the part of my family. Across from me are Jamey, the Number-three Chan son, and Coolie, who plays *his* family. Number-three Chan son and I have never seen each other, but this evening we shall be married because our families have ordered it. I have heard that in some modern Chinese families, the sons and daughters themselves choose the people they wish to marry, but in our family it has never been this way."

Charlotte turned and pointed to Amah Cho Mei, who bowed to the audience. "Seven months ago, a friend of my oldest aunt became the go-between who spoke to my parents of Number-three Chan son. The go-between," said Charlotte, as Amah walked back and forth between Coolie and Dossafoo, pretending to speak to each, "visits my family, telling them of the merits of Number-three Chan son, and then visits the Chan family, telling them the merits of me, Number-two Ling daughter. The go-between is very happy because both families agree that she has made a good choice for each of them."

Smiling, Amah Cho Mei bowed again to the audience. As she did, Dossafoo and Coolie left their posts by Charlotte and Jamey and went to the far end of the veranda, where they seated themselves behind a table. Amah walked toward them.

"The names of the young couple," said Charlotte, "together with the year, month, day, and hour of their births, are given to wise-men astrologers to see if the signs are good for them to be married."

Dossafoo and Coolie pretended to consult with each other, then nodded to Amah.

"The signs are good," announced Charlotte. "This means that Number-three Chan son and I will have the very best good fortune if we marry!"

"Hurrah!" shouted Cousin Philip. Everyone applauded laughingly, and Jamey, forgetting that he was part of the performance, applauded, too. This brought more laughter and applause from the audience.

Charlotte smiled warmly at her cousin and was thrilled to have him return the smile.

"Now," she continued, "the parents of the future groom must send presents to the home of my family."

Coolie hurried into the living room, returning with a small table on which were drinking glasses set upside down.

"These glasses," Charlotte explained, "represent glass boxes containing precious ornaments. Because the Chan family is very rich, they are able to send one ornament of jade, which is a symbol of good luck." She lifted up one glass, showing a green glass salt shaker under it. "See this beautiful jade vase!"

The audience "ooohed" and "aaahed" its approval.

"The date of the marriage is fixed now by letter—and it must be written on red paper—from the Chan family to the Ling family," Charlotte said.

Coolie lifted a folded piece of red paper from behind a pillow on Jamey's chair and delivered it to Dossafoo. When he had returned to Jamey, he picked up another piece of red paper, displaying a fierce dragon drawn by Charlotte. At the same time, Dossafoo held up a piece of green paper, showing the picture of a phoenix, or at least the closest thing to a phoenix Charlotte could draw.

"Pictures of a dragon on red paper from the boy's family, and of a phoenix on green paper from the girl's family, are then exchanged," Charlotte said, as Dossafoo and Coolie each handed the other the pictures. "These are really letters telling about the boy and the girl. Also, with the red dragon letter, the boy's family gives gifts, one of which must be a goose."

Coolie now held up a large cardboard box on which Charlotte had written in Oriental-style English letters the words "Goose and Other Presents," and gave it to Dossafoo. Charlotte had to wait a few moments for the audience to stop laughing once they'd read the words on the box.

Then she said, "At last, it's the wedding day. All the invitations to the wedding have been sent out, and there have been many presents of scrolls, wine, food, clothes, and money. Money is the best because it helps to pay for the wedding."

"Hear, hear!" said Mr. Barrett, and Charlotte frowned at him.

"All the presents and the bride's dowry are now being taken to the bride's new home. My family, the Ling family, is very wealthy, so they have had to hire two hundred men to carry all the presents!" Charlotte said proudly.

As Charlotte spoke, Dossafoo ran back and forth from the living room, each time bringing out a new object—a scroll, an oil lamp, a quilted blanket, and a small table—taking all these things to Coolie on the Chan side of the veranda.

"Now," said Charlotte, "everything is ready, and it's time for the wedding chair to leave in a procession from the bridegroom's home to bring back the bride."

With this announcement, Dossafoo and Coolie hurried into the living room and returned in a moment, carrying what looked like a real wedding sedan chair. Charlotte, with the help of Dossafoo and Coolie, had lashed bamboo poles to a wicker chair so that it could be carried like a sedan chair. She had also lashed four smaller upright bamboo poles to the chair and draped a red cotton curtain over them so that the occupant of the sedan chair would be completely hidden. On the curtain she had pinned red geraniums from their garden and pieces of gold paper cut into swirls and curlicues. Amah Cho Mei had found enough embroidery thread in her sewing basket to make four tassels, and Charlotte had hung them from the four top corners of the chair.

As soon as the sedan chair appeared on the scene, the small audience applauded wildly.

"Chris," Charlotte heard her mother say, "when did Charlie do all that?"

"She's been working on it all along in Amah's room," Christene replied, rather proudly, Charlotte thought.

"Well!" said Mrs. Barrett.

"It's just lovely, isn't it?" Miss Bell said.

"Very clever, these American-Chinese young ladies!" Cousin Philip replied.

"Oh, Philip," Mrs. Barrett said, laughing.

Charlotte felt as if she could float right off the veranda. It wasn't until Amah Cho Mei had climbed into the sedan chair at the back of the veranda, and then climbed back out again in front of her, that Charlotte remembered with a start that the wedding was still going on, and she wasn't finished yet.

"This is the ch'u ch'in t'ai t'ai, the marriage dame," she hurried to explain. "She has come to place the veil over my face and to take me to the home of the bridegroom."

After pinning a red carnation into Charlotte's hair, Amah Cho Mei drew from her pocket a piece of red embroidered silk with blue lining and tassels, and placed it over Charlotte's head.

"As you can see," said Charlotte, "ch'u ch'in t'ai t'ai has covered my face entirely. Now, except for her, *no one* can see my face except the bridegroom when he lifts the veil and sees it for the very first time! Ch'u ch'in t'ai t'ai now helps me into the red sedan chair. In a real wedding, there would also be a green sedan chair for her to ride in to the bridegroom's house. Tonight you'll have to imagine one. After ch'u ch'in t'ai t'ai and I are safely in our chairs, the procession returns to the groom's house."

With Amah Cho Mei following behind, Dossafoo and Coolie lifted the sedan chair and, with Charlotte hidden behind its red curtain, marched twice around the veranda, stopping finally several feet from Jamey. As soon as the sedan chair had been set down, Dossafoo picked up three sticks of bamboo from the floor and threw them down at the foot of the chair.

"One of the male guests has thrown arrows at the sedan chair in order to drive away evil spirits they may have met on the road," Charlotte explained from inside the chair. "Now you see ch'u ch'in t'ai t'ai lift up the curtain of my chair and hand me an apple. I must take a bite from the apple, put the bite into my hand, and throw it on the floor. After this, ch'u ch'in t'ai t'ai puts a spot of red paint on each of my cheeks as a sign that I am now a married woman. She gives me a gift of a vase containing rice, millet, and some jewelry. Now she helps me out of the chair and along a carpet of red felt to the room where the groom is waiting."

They were coming to the most important part of the wedding, where Jamey, the groom, lifted the veil to see the face of Charlotte, his bride, for the very first time. In all the rehearsals, Jamey had giggled every single time he'd done it, and Charlotte was in despair over him. But there had seemed to be nothing she could do about it.

Led by Amah Cho Mei, Charlotte walked slowly toward Jamey and stood with her hands folded, waiting. Then Jamey, who had to stand on his tiptoes to do it, lifted her veil. And when Charlotte saw his face, she knew that the last moments of the wedding perform- ance would be a success. Jamey looked just as serious and solemn as he had when, somewhere months before in the middle of Chinese City, he had folded his hands to say, "Sheh sheh, lao shen shung!"

As Charlotte explained in almost a whisper what they were doing, she and Jamey turned and bowed to a picture of T'ien Ti Wand, the god of heaven and earth. Then they made silent toasts to one another with ceremonial cups of wine and acted out the eating of dumplings brought from the bride's home and served to them by ch'u ch'in t'ai t'ai.

When all this was finished, Charlotte and Jamey rose from the ceremonial table and bowed to the au- dience as Charlotte said, "Number-two Ling daughter

and Number-three Chan son are now man and wife, according to the ancient and honorable customs of China!"

And it was all over!

Applause rang out from the darkened veranda, sounding as if it came from fifty people instead of only seven.

"Bravo! Bravo!" Mr. Barrett called out.

"Curtain call! Curtain call!" Cousin Philip shouted. "Where did the rest of the cast and crew disappear?"

Amah Cho Mei, Dossafoo, and Coolie had rushed into the living room as soon as the performance was over, and now they stood peering through the doorway, beaming at everyone. Charlotte and Jamey ran over to them and tried to pull them onto the veranda, but they were too shy and wouldn't come. So Cousin Philip ran over to them, shaking Dossafoo and Coolie's hands and bowing to Amah, who giggled behind her hands like a young girl.

"So this is what you and Anna were up to," Miss Bell said.

"Some of the time," Charlotte said happily.

"Well then, I think that all of it was worthwhile. Oh, I do wish Anna could have been here tonight. Just think how she would have felt, seeing you act out so cleverly all the things she told you!"

"A very smart girl, this Charlie!" Cousin Philip said, putting his arm around Charlotte's shoulders. Then he winked at Miss Bell and her friends, Mr. and Mrs. Carney, who were standing beside her. "You didn't know you were acquiring a charming, talented cousin right along with me, did you, Pat?"

There was an immediate silence on the veranda. Mr.

212

Barrett looked questioningly at Cousin Philip. "What was *that* remark all about, Philip?"

And then Charlotte's glory was over. In less than thirty seconds, entirely over! Cousin Philip's arm left her shoulders, his other arm slipped around Miss Bell, and Charlotte heard him say, "Well, with all this wedding business in the air, Pat and I decided this might be a good time to announce another wedding—*ours!*"

"Oh, Pat!" Mrs. Barrett rushed over to Miss Bell and hugged her. "And Philip! How marvelous!"

"Philip, you devil!" Mr. Barrett said, shaking his cousin's hand so hard he seemed intent on breaking it. "You really kept this to yourself!"

"Chris, Charlie, Jamey! Come welcome Miss Bell into the family!" Mrs. Barrett said. "Oh, this is truly wonderful news, both of you!"

The only one of the three of them who went to Miss Bell was Christene. She was blushing furiously and smiling a funny kind of half smile, but at least she did go. Jamey just threw his arms around Amah Cho Mei and hid his face in her jacket, while Charlotte did nothing at all. Embarrassed and miserable, she felt like a ridiculous lump just standing there, but what was she supposed to do?

In the matter of a moment, Charlotte's play had been dismissed from everyone's mind, along with Charlotte herself, like a child dismissed from a room, with the conversation going right on as if the child had never been there at all. But worst of all, in the matter of a moment, Cousin Philip, who had called Charlotte charming and talented and who had given her disarmingly special smiles when she'd been acting on the stage in front of him—Cousin Philip, for whom the whole wedding performance had really been given, was no longer *her* Cousin Philip. All in the matter of a terrible moment, that was over.

The charming, talented, important, special Charlotte suddenly became the awkward, string beany, in-need-of-orthodontia Charlotte, and exactly what she was, eleven years old going on twelve. So what was she supposed to do? Smile and say polite things? Apparently yes!

Jamey was sent off to bed after a brief appearance from behind Amah Cho Mei's jacket, but Charlotte, along with Christene, had to stay on the veranda for another long hour. She had to suffer through being asked what she thought of this wonderful news, and being told that now they were to call Miss Bell "Pat," though Charlotte couldn't see what difference this last point made. No matter what they called her, she had become a stranger now. Charlotte had to listen endlessly to this Pat bubbling over about Cousin Philip and their silly wedding plans. But probably the worst insult of all was having Cousin Philip, of all people, ask her that horrible question that grown-ups ask *children*, "Has the cat got your tongue, Charlie?" It was the most degrading moment of the evening.

Charlotte noticed, however, that nobody asked Christene that question, though she seemed equally quiet. Well, why would they? She hadn't just finished "entertaining" the grown-ups with a babyish performance.

The hour ended, and Mrs. Barrett finally suggested that Charlotte had had a busy day and that she, but not Christene, of course, ought to go to bed. Ordinarily, Charlotte would have argued, but tonight she was glad

214

to escape. As she was leaving, Miss Bell—Pat—did remember to say again how wonderful she thought the performance was. Then everyone else chimed in to say the same thing, but nobody's mind seemed to be really on it. Charlotte could hear them, as soon as she'd left, back on the subject of the wedding again. Only it wasn't hers.

She trailed off to her room, flopped down on her bed, and began dragging off one shoe, then the other, and finally, the faded beach coat that had been her costume in the play. She threw it down on the floor, never wanting to see it again.

She was still undressing when the door opened and, surprisingly, Christene walked in. She had thought that Christene, to assert her grown-up superiority if nothing else, would have stayed on the veranda another half hour at least.

"Is Cousin Philip taking Miss Bell home already?" Charlotte asked, determinedly not saying "Pat."

"No, he isn't," Christene replied. She opened her dresser drawer, but only stared down into it without removing anything. She sounded curt, abrupt, and annoyed. With Charlotte? Charlotte couldn't bear any more. With her undershirt halfway over her head, her nose muffled in cotton lisle, she burst into tears.

"Now what's wrong?" Christene said sharply.

"Nothing!" said Charlotte, sobbing into her shirt.

She heard the drawer pushed quietly shut.

"Charlie, what is it?"

Charlotte pulled the shirt over her head and dived down onto her pillow. "My play was so babyish. It was so babyish, Chrissy!"

"No, it wasn't, Charlie. It really wasn't. *I* liked it. Everybody did."

Charlotte picked at the tufts on her bedspread and kept on sniffling.

"Charlie, I *said* they all liked it. They talked about it after you'd left. You're just being stupid to cry about it."

"Chrissy, it isn't just the play. It's that—it's that—Chrissy, why does Cousin Philip have to go and get married!"

For a moment there was silence. "Well, I suppose he has to sometime," Christene said abruptly.

"Yes, but why couldn't he have waited a few years?"

There was further silence.

"For you?" Christene said simply. "Were you planning to marry him, Charlie?"

Charlotte looked up at her sister in surprise and felt her face grow hot. It was such a deeply kept secret that she hardly admitted it to herself, but at the age of six she had calmly and matter-of-factly determined that she would marry Cousin Philip one day, and she hadn't changed her mind since. Slowly, she nodded her head in answer to Christene's question.

"Well, if you must know, Charlie, so was I." Christene, leaning against the dresser with her pajamas clutched in her hands, stared rigidly at the floor.

"But I thought it was"—Charlotte hesitated—"I thought it was Moira Evans who was—"

"She was!" said Christene. "We *both* were!" And then, strangely and unaccountably, she began to giggle.

"What's funny?" asked Charlotte, growing more surprised by the minute.

"Moira Evans thought Cousin Philip was going to marry her right then, when she was still in the eighth grade!" Christene exploded with laughter.

"In the eighth grade?" Charlotte squealed.

"Yes!" Christene was laughing so hard now that her voice came out in a squeak. This sent the two of them off into fresh gales of laughter, and Christene finally crashed down on her bed as if she couldn't stand up any longer.

"But—but—Charlie, do you remember that snaky woman at Mother and Daddy's party that Moira and I"—Christene gasped for air—"Moira and I went to?"

Charlotte nodded. "The long stringy one in green Georgette who looked like a sea serpent?"

"Yes, that one," wheezed Christene. "Well, she was draping herself all over Cousin Philip half the evening, and Mother said later that *she* was planning to marry him. She actually told Mother!"

"She didn't!"

"She did!"

"Well, that—that makes four of us going to marry him!"

"At least!" said Christene, and they both screeched with merriment.

"I wonder how many more there were?" Charlotte said happily.

"Thousands!" groaned Christene, and they were off again.

Tears running down their cheeks, helpless with laughter, they threw themselves backwards on their beds, giggling hysterically, quieting down for a few moments until one of them would groan again, and then they would both shriek with laughter once more.

At last, when they had said all the funny things they could think of to say about it, and lay exhausted from laughter, Charlotte said, "Well, I guess he's going to marry Miss Dumpymouse."

Christene crossed her hands over her pajamas and stared at the ceiling. "She's not Miss Dumpymouse, Charlie."

"I thought you thought she was."

"That was a long time ago. She's really nice, I guess. Anyway, I thought *you* liked her."

"I did."

"Don't you still?"

"Yes," said Charlotte.

"Well, anyway, she's going to be our cousin."

"Yes, she is," said Charlotte, and there seemed to be nothing else to say about it.

Finally, Christene sat up in bed and began pulling off her socks. "I'm tired, Charlie. Let's go to bed."

"All right," said Charlotte agreeably, though she would have liked to go on talking.

But once Christene had pulled off her socks, she didn't do anything more toward getting ready for bed. She remained sitting up in bed, knees drawn up under her chin, apparently engrossed by the sight of her toes, because she kept staring at them, and staring at them.

"Charlie?"

"What, Chrissy?"

"Charlie, I don't think I want to go away to boarding school this year."

For a moment, Charlotte was too stunned to say anything. Christene had been desperate to go away, Charlotte thought, and when given the choice of remaining in Tientsin and going to the British high school, or going away to Peking to the American boarding school, Christene had chosen Peking immediately.

But more than that, it was a subject she had never before discussed with Charlotte. Most of what Charlotte
knew about it, she had learned from their mother and
father.

"But, Chrissy, I thought you *wanted* to go."

"I did. I don't anymore."

"Oh," said Charlotte, adding after a moment, "Have
you talked about it to Mother and Daddy?"

"Yes. They said it's too late to change my mind now.
The arrangements have already been made. They said
that, *you* know, that I'd—"

"Get over it!" Charlotte finished for her. Yes, she
certainly did know. That had been said to *her* often
enough. "But, Chrissy," she said quickly, "you'll get to
come home for the holidays, and in October for Cousin
Philip and Miss Bell—*Pat's* wedding. They might ask
us to be bridesmaids."

"Yes, I suppose they might," Christene said.

"And you'll have your old room when you come
home, Chris. I won't go into it while you're gone, I
promise."

After a long silence, Christene said, "It won't be my
room anymore. Mother wants it for a sewing room, and
I said it would be all right. I suppose I'll be in the playroom with you when I come home."

"Won't you mind?" Charlotte asked.

"I don't think so. Why? Will you?"

"Christmas is better in the same room," said
Charlotte.

"Yes, it is," said Christene.

"It will be Christmas soon, Chrissy, and you'll be
home, and we can open our stockings together. We can
always do that together, can't we?"

"For ten whole years?" Christene said.

"Fifty!" said Charlotte.

"One hundred?"

"A thousand!"

"One million?"

"At least!" said Charlotte.

"Oh, at least, Charlie!" Christene said, and then they both laughed because when they had played this game as little girls, they had really believed it could happen.

Too wide awake to fall asleep, Charlotte hugged her pillow, thinking over the game they had just played, the day that had just ended. It had been a strange day, one minute up, one minute down. Like her whole year, Charlotte thought, where she'd been happy one moment, miserable the next, wanting to remain a little girl, and yet not wanting to at the very same time.

And now she knew that it was that way for Christene, too, that things had never been so simple for her sister as she'd supposed. She thought of Christene putting polish on her nails, but wanting a doll for Christmas; Christene so worldly wise on the subject of hairdos and parties, but wanting to raise a family of baby mice in her dresser drawer. Christene had wanted to do it all along, Charlotte realized now, but raising mice in your dresser wasn't a very grown-up thing to do, so she had needed Charlotte to make the decision. That way, she could feel she was doing it only to please Charlotte, not herself.

Now Christene didn't want to go away to school! And the most surprising thing was that she had turned to Charlotte for comfort. But not so surprising after all—because we've become friends again, thought Charlotte.

You might replace something lost with something else, but it would never be the same as the thing that was gone, their father had said. That might be true, but wasn't it also true that the thing lost might be replaced with something better? Wasn't Christene's and her friendship better now, just as Anna's and her friendship was going to be? Wouldn't they be able to share things now that they had never shared before?

"Chrissy?" Charlotte whispered.

"Yes?"

"Are you asleep?"

"Not yet."

"Chrissy—"

"What is it, Charlie?"

"I wonder if I'm pretty enough to be in a wedding? Do you think I am?"

"People don't get asked to be in weddings just because they're pretty, Charlie."

"I know that," said Charlotte. "I just want to know if *you* think I am."

There was a long silence.

"You're you, Charlie. That's enough. But if you want to know something else, I heard Cousin Philip telling Mother once that we were both going to be beauties when we grew up."

"*Both* of us?"

"Both of us."

"Are you sure he meant me?"

"He didn't mean Jamey, dummy!"

"Oh," said Charlotte. Then after a few moments, "Well, it will be a long time before I start growing up."

"Don't be silly," Christene said, yawning. "You've already started."

Before Charlotte could think of any more questions to ask on the subject, she heard the soft, steady breathing that told her Christene had fallen asleep.

It's all right, Charlotte thought. It may not be all right next week or next month or next year, but there will always be a moment when it is all right, when everything is all right, just as it is now. As for tomorrow? Well, tomorrow she would simply be a day older. And a day more grown-up. Funny not to know something like that, but Christene had said, "You've already started," so she supposed she had. Am I ready, Charlotte wondered, to like what might happen to me tomorrow, and all the tomorrows after that?

For a long time, she lay listening to the soft, comforting sounds of grown-ups talking and laughing in the background, the hushed whispering of the waves washing over the sand at the foot of the cliff, the familiar sound of her sister's steady breathing in the bed beside her. And as she listened, she puzzled how things could have happened to her that she hadn't even noticed happening.

"You've already started," Christene had said, but there was something else. "You're you, Charlie," she had also said. And that seemed to be the answer to all of it. Whatever had happened yesterday or today, or would happen tomorrow, she was still Charlotte, and could go right on being Charlotte, just as Christene had really gone right on being Christene.

So, yes, Charlotte decided at last, in that case I think I will like what happens to me tomorrow. Tomorrow I will be ready to like it. And in a few moments, like her sister, she was asleep.

About the Author

BARBARA BROOKS WALLACE knows the China she writes about in this book, for, like Missy Charlie, she was born in China and spent her childhood there. Her father was an American businessman and her mother had been a nurse in Shanghai, where they met and married. Mrs. Wallace was born in Soochow, China.

As foreign children in China, she writes, she and her sister "lived a petted, pampered kind of life. There were often strange and frightening things happening all around us—terrible epidemics, Chinese inexplicably corralled to have their heads whacked off in the middle of the street, a factory uprising under our window, soldiers marching —but somehow we always felt safe and protected from all of it, as if we were fenced off by some kind of invisible magic circle. Perhaps children always feel that way no matter where they live—that nothing really bad can ever happen to them. Or, for that matter, that nothing very exciting ever happens to them, either!"

While in China, she and her sister were "always closely guarded by amahs and Mother, but the first time Mother ever let us out of her sight—which was to allow us to leave Shanghai under the care of a lady missionary doctor to spend the summer in Peitaho—the 'unofficial' Japanese war flared up and we were totally cut off from Shanghai. Mother and Dad were evacuated to the Philippines from Shanghai, and later, my sister and I were evacuated from Peitaho on an American destroyer."

Mrs. Wallace attended schools in China and had crossed the Pacific nine times before coming to live in the United States. After graduating from the University of California at Los Angeles, she did promotional work for an advertising agency and later became assistant to a manager of a radio station. She now lives with her husband, a former air force officer, and their teen-age son, Jimmy, in Alexandria, Virginia.